# COLLINS

# Toddler Playtime

*Illustrated by Sam Williams*

Collins

*An Imprint of HarperCollinsPublishers*

If you enjoy TODDLER PLAYTIME,
you'll love TODDLER BEDTIME too!

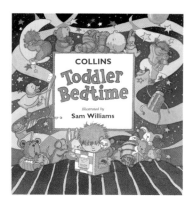

Available in hardback, paperback and book & tape

First published in Great Britain by HarperCollins Publishers Ltd in 1998

1 3 5 7 9 10 8 6 4 2

ISBN: 0 00 198291-5

Compilation copyright © HarperCollins Publishers Ltd 1998

Illustrations copyright © Sam Williams 1998

Text copyright, as follows:

Here Comes Rosie!; It's Time for Lunch, Rosie! © Tony Bradman 1998

Jack in the Bag © Lisa Bruce 1998

The Park © Trish Cooke 1998

The Little One Dresses Up © Alan Durant 1998

Harry's Party © Vivian French 1998

Make a Face © Tony Mitton 1998

Daisy Likes Helping © Rachel Pank 1998

The authors and illustrator assert the moral right to be identified as the authors and illustrator of the work.

A CIP catalogue for this title is available from the British Library.

Printed in Singapore by Imago.

# CONTENTS

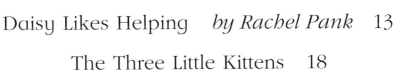

# RING-A-RING O' ROSES

Ring-a-ring o' roses,
A pocket full of posies,
A-tishoo, a-tishoo,
We all fall down.

The king has sent his daughter
To fetch a pail of water,
A-tishoo, a-tishoo,
We all fall down.

The robin on the steeple
Is singing to the people,
A-tishoo, a-tishoo,
We all fall down.

# HERE COMES ROSIE!

Rosie's learning how to walk...
Stand back – there she goes!
Toddling through the doorway
On her tippy-toes.

Wobbling past the sofa,
Arms up in the air,
Round and round the table,
Bouncing off a chair.

Staggering to the left a bit...
Treading on a tail!
Staggering to the right a bit...
Steady... grab that rail!

She heads off for the pot plants,
And she breaks into a run...
*Here comes Rosie!*
Walking is such... *FUN!*

*Tony Bradman*

# JACK IN THE BAG

*by Lisa Bruce*

Jack was fed up.

"This box is too square," he grumbled. "It's boring. I don't want to live here any more." He opened the lid, sprang out with a mighty

**BOINNG**

and set off in search of a new home.

Jack landed near a big red ball.

"That's not square," he said. "I know, I can be a 'Jack on the Ball'. That's the perfect home for me."

Jack jumped on top, but the ball wibbled and wobbled and rolled right over.

"I don't think this is a good home after all," said Jack, rubbing his head. "It doesn't stay still."

By the wall was a big bed.

"That looks like it will stay still," grinned Jack. "Yes! I can be a 'Jack in the Bed'. That's the perfect home for me."

Jack jumped up, but when he tried to bounce he got tangled in the quilt.

"I don't think this is a good home after all," said Jack, frowning. "I can't jump properly."

Beside the bed was a bin.

"I can bounce properly in there," said Jack. "I can be a 'Jack in the Bin'. That's the perfect home for me."

Jack jumped in, but the bin was full of apple cores and crumpled paper.

"I don't think this is a good home after all," said Jack, wrinkling up his nose. "It's much too messy."

Just then, Jack heard a swooshing from the bathroom.

"That's nice and clean," said Jack. "I can be a 'Jack in the Bath'. That must be the perfect home for me."

Jack jumped over, but the bath was full of water and the water was wet.

"I don't think this is a good home after all," Jack spluttered. "My spring will get rusty."

On the floor Jack saw a straw bag.

"That looks dry," said Jack. "I can be a 'Jack in the Bag'. At last I've found the perfect home for me."

Jack jumped through the straps. He tried to snuggle down but there were books everywhere.

"Oh dear, I don't think this is such a good home after all," said Jack, squirming. "It's just not comfortable."

In a corner of the room was a square box.
It was clean and tidy. It was dry, it stayed still
and it looked just right for bouncing.

"Hum..." thought Jack.

**BOINNG**

Jack jumped inside and closed the lid.

"Ah," sighed Jack, with a smile.
"This is just right. I think I'll be a
'Jack in the Box'. This really *is* the
best home for me."

Choo, Choo, Choo

# DOWN BY THE STATION

Down by the station, early in the morning,
See the little puffer trains all in a row.
See the engine driver pull the little handle.
Choo, choo, choo, and off we go.

Chug,
Chug, Chug

Down at the farmyard, early in the morning,
See the little tractor standing in the barn.
Do you see the farmer pull the little handle?
Chug, chug, chug, and off we go.

Down in the harbour, early in the morning,
See the little tugboats bobbing up and down.
Do you see the captain pull the little handle?
Toot, toot, toot, and off we go.

toot, toot, toot

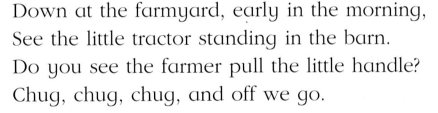

# MAKE A FACE

I can make a fat face,
a dog face, a cat face.
I can make a thin face,
a skinny little pin face.
I can made a mad face,
a horrid, mean and bad face,
a sick face, a sad face,
a rather like my Dad face.
I can make a funny face,
a just as sweet as honey face.
I can make a happy face,
a sharp snarl and snappy face.
I can make a true face,
a just for me and you face.
But this face,
you ain't seen this face –
NO PLACE!

*Tony Mitton*

# DAISY LIKES HELPING

## by Rachel Pank

Daddy was busy washing up.

"That looks like fun," thought
Daisy, as she watched him splashing about with his big
yellow gloves in the soapy water. She tugged at Daddy's
jumper.

"Can I help?" she asked.

"If you're very careful," said Dad, and he fetched Daisy's
stool. They squeezed together at the sink and Daisy happily
sploshed and splished with her sponge.

"I like helping," said Daisy.

But very soon Dad had water and bubbles all over his
jumper and he was shouting,

"Watch those plates, Daisy!"

Too late, CRASH! a plate fell and broke into pieces on the
wet floor.

"Why don't you go and help
Mummy now?" said Dad.

Daisy found Mum in the hall,
painting the walls a nice new
sunny yellow.

"Mummy, can I help?" asked
Daisy. Mum was not too sure.

"Well..." she said, "painting
is very messy."

"But I like helping," said Daisy.

"OK, if you're very careful,"
said Mum, and she put on
Daisy's apron.

Soon Daisy wanted to
have a go up the ladder.
One step... two steps...

"STOP!" shouted Mum,
"and careful with that brush!"

Too late, PLOP! a big blob
of yellow paint landed on Mum's nose.
Daisy didn't notice.

"I *like* helping," she declared.
Just then, the doorbell rang. It was Grandma.

Grandma looked at Daisy's wet and soapy Dad and at
Daisy's yellow and splodgy Mum.

"What's been going on here?" she laughed.

"Daisy has been HELPING!" said Mum and Dad together.

"I **like** helping," said Daisy, beaming at Grandma.

"I'll tell you what," Grandma said, lifting Daisy down from
the ladder. "I've got lots of cakes to make and I need
somebody to help me."

Daisy jumped up and down. "Me, me, ME! I like helping!"

So off Daisy went to Grandma's house to make some cakes, leaving Mum and Dad and lots of mess behind her.

Daisy helped Grandma to break the eggs. CRACK! an egg rolled to the floor.

"It doesn't matter," said Grandma.

Then Daisy mixed in the flour.

"Grandma, your hair's gone white," said Daisy, when the flour went everywhere.

"Never mind," said Grandma. Together they put the cake mixture into little paper bun cases.

"Yummy," said Daisy, licking butter and sugar off her chin.

AT LAST, the cakes were finished and Grandma put them in
the oven to bake. Daisy looked around at the mess.

"Grandma, your kitchen needs cleaning up!" she said.
"But I'm a bit too tired to help now!"

"Never mind," smiled Grandma, lifting Daisy on to her lap.
"But there is just one last thing I'd like you to help me do."

"What is it, Grandma?" asked Daisy.

Grandma laughed. "You can help me to eat some cakes!"

Daisy smiled happily. "I LOVE helping!" she said.

# THE THREE LITTLE KITTENS

Three little kittens, they lost their mittens
And they began to cry,
"Oh, mother dear, see here, see here,
Our mittens we have lost."
"What, lost your mittens?
You naughty kittens!
Then you shall have no pie."
*Me-ow! Me-ow! Me-ow! Me-ow!*

Three little kittens, they found their mittens
And they began to cry,
"Oh, mother dear, see here, see here,
Our mittens we have found."
"What, found your mittens?
You darling kittens!
Then you shall have some pie."
*Me-ow! Me-ow! Me-ow! Me-ow!*

Three little kittens put on their mittens
And soon ate up the pie.
"Oh, mother dear, we greatly fear,
Our mittens we have soiled."
"What, soiled your mittens?
You naughty kittens!"
And they began to sigh.
*Me-ow! Me-ow! Me-ow! Me-ow!*

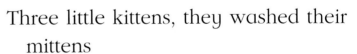

Three little kittens, they washed their
  mittens
And hung them up to dry.
"Oh, mother dear, see here, see here,
Our mittens we have washed."
"What, washed your mittens?
You darling kittens!
But I smell a mouse close by!"
*Hush! Hush! Hush! Hush!*

*Eliza Lee Follen*

19

# IT'S TIME FOR LUNCH, ROSIE!

Rosie's got her bib on,
She's got a cup and spoon,
She's sitting in her high chair –
Her lunch is coming soon!

Something very tasty,
Food she loves to eat,
Though first she has to mix it up...
And drop it on her feet!

Then she has to spread it out
And smear it on her tray,
Then she dabs it on her hair...
And throws her spoon away!

Now her bowl is empty.
What does Rosie say?
"Food all gone! Let me out!
*Rosie wants to play!*"

*Tony Bradman*

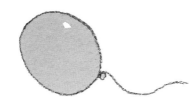

# HARRY'S PARTY

*by Vivian French*

On Monday, Harry had a letter.

"What does it say?" Harry asked Mum.

"It's from Kate," Mum said. "She's having a party."

"Good," said Harry. "I like parties. Is the party today?"

"No," said Mum. "It's on Thursday."

On Tuesday, Harry was busy with his crayons and a piece of paper.

"I'm making Kate a birthday card," he said.

"It's lovely," Mum said.

On Wednesday, Harry and Mum went to the toy shop.

"What do you think Kate would like?" Mum asked Harry.

"I want a torch," Harry said. "Then I could shine it in the dark."

"Shall we get a torch for Kate?" Mum suggested.

"And for me too," said Harry. "I want a red one."

Mum shook her head. "It's not your birthday, Harry."

On Thursday morning, Harry wrapped up Kate's torch.

"I wish it was mine," he said.

"I'm sure Kate will like it very much," Mum said.

After lunch, Harry put on his clean clothes. He picked up the present and the card, and he and Mum walked down the road to Kate's house. Mum rang the bell, and Kate's Mum opened the door.

"Hullo, Harry!" she said. Kate rushed up. "Hullo!"

"Hullo," said Harry. "Here's your present. It's a torch. If you don't like it, I don't mind. I like it lots, and I can take it home." But Kate was jumping up and down. "A torch! I LOVE torches!" She ripped off the paper. "THANK YOU!"

"Oh," said Harry.

Harry was very quiet when everyone else was playing musical bumps. He didn't eat much at tea time. He didn't want to pin the tail on the donkey.

"Are you all right, Harry?" Kate's Mum asked.

"Yes," said Harry.

"Good," said Kate's Mum. "Because we're going to play pass the parcel!"

"Oh," said Harry.

Everyone sat down in a circle. The parcel went round and round, and when the music stopped someone pulled off a layer of paper. There were sweets inside, and Kate and the other children laughed and grabbed to get a turn. Only Harry sat quietly. The music got louder, and the parcel went round again and again.

"STOP!" called Kate's Mum. The music stopped.

"Come on, Harry," Kate said. "You've got the parcel!"

"Oh," said Harry. He slowly took off a layer of paper. Inside was a box.

"OPEN IT!" shouted Kate. "OPEN IT!" Harry opened the box.

"OH!" he said. "OH! OH! OH!" Inside was a torch. A red torch.

"WOW!" said Harry.

When Mum came to collect Harry he was being the noisiest of all the children.

"Was it a good party?" she asked.

"It was the BEST party I've EVER been to," Harry said, and he shone his torch all the way home.

# THE PARK

Push me mama
Push me high
Push me up
Make me reach the sky!
I won't scream mama
I won't cry
Just push me high mama
Push me high!

Push me round mama
Push me round
'Til both my feet
Cannot touch the ground
Make me spin mama
Make me turn
'Til inside my belly
Go 'squiggle and squirm'!

Push me down mama
Let go my hand
Let me whizz to the bottom
Let me roll down and land
Whoiiiiiii mama
Do it again
Wheeeeeeeeee
I like that game!

*Trish Cooke*

25

# OVER IN THE MEADOW

Over in the meadow, in the sand, in the sun,
Lived an old mother frog and her little froggie, one.
"Croak," said the mother.
"I croak," said the one.
So they croaked and they croaked in the sand, in the sun.

Over in the meadow, in the stream so blue,
Lived an old mother fish and her little fishes, two.
"Swim!" said the mother.
"We swim," said the two.
So they swam and they swam in the stream so blue.

Over in the meadow, on a branch of the tree,
Lived an old mother bird and her little birdies, three.
"Sing," said the mother.
"We sing," said the three.
So they sang and they sang on a branch of the tree.

# THE LITTLE ONE DRESSES UP
## *by Alan Durant*

The children were playing dressing-up games.

Matthew was the king and Kelly was the queen. The twins, Drew and Daisy, were the prince and princess.

"You can be our puppy," they said to the Little One.

"Don't want to be a puppy," growled the Little One. "I want to be a princess."

"You can't, I'm the princess," said Daisy. "I'll let you play with my ball."

"OK," said the Little One, and she ran around the playroom on all fours, going, "Woof woof, woof woof."

For a while all went well. The royal family played happily in the palace with their puppy – until the puppy bit the princess on the bottom. The princess howled and howled... and the puppy was sent to her kennel in disgrace.

When the Little One had said sorry, she was allowed to play again. The game was mummies and daddies now. Kelly was the mummy, Matthew was the daddy, and the twins were the little boy and girl.

"You can be our baby," they told the Little One.

"Don't want to be a baby," said the Little One. "I want to be big."

"We'll tuck you up in the cot and sing to you," soothed Kelly.

"OK," said the Little One, and she climbed into the cot and went, "Gagagagaga, babababa."

For a while the family was very happy. The mummy,

daddy, and the little boy and girl sang to the baby and kissed her and tickled her. The baby snorted and gurgled and got very excited – *too* excited. A large wet patch appeared.

"Eugh," cried Drew. "She's done a wee."

The Little One had to go off to get cleaned up and changed.

When she returned, the others were playing animals. Matthew was a lion, Kelly was a tiger and the twins were foxes.

"You can be Chicken Licken," they said to the Little One, "and we'll eat you up."

"Don't want to be a chicken," said the Little One. "I want to be a tiger."

"You're too small," said Matthew, and he roared a terrible tiger's roar, "ROARRR!"

The Little One ran away.

She ran and hid in the bathroom cupboard and buried herself under a sheet. She sat in the darkness feeling cross.

Outside, the lion and the tiger and the little foxes crept closer, growling and prowling, until they came to the cupboard door. There was a moment of silent stillness, then the door whooshed open.

The Little One raised her arms under the sheet.

"Aaaah!" cried the others. "Help! It's a ghost!"

The Little One stood up and waved her arms.

"Oooooooo!" she wailed. "Oooooo!"

"Quick, run!" the others screamed. And they ran away, with the ghost chasing after them.

They ended up in a giggling heap on the playroom floor.

"That was a good game," said Matthew breathlessly.

"Let's all be ghosts!" cried Kelly.

So they all put sheets over their heads and chased each other round the room, moaning and wailing. This time the Little One didn't have to be a puppy or a baby or a chicken. She didn't have to be anything little at all. She was just a ghost like all the others and it was GREAT fun!

31

# ONE, TWO, THREE, FOUR, FIVE

1 2 3 4 5

One, two, three, four, five,
Once I caught a fish alive;
Six, seven, eight, nine, ten,
Then I let him go again.
Why did you let him go?
Because he bit my finger so;
Which finger did he bite?
This little finger on my right.

# The BRADMAN ERA

# The BRADMAN ERA

RECALLED BY
**BILL O'REILLY**

COMPILED BY
**JACK EGAN**

**Willow Books**
Collins
8 Grafton Street, London W1
1984

Willow Books
William Collins Sons & Co Ltd
London · Glasgow · Sydney · Auckland
Toronto · Johannesburg

First published jointly in Australia in 1983
by the Australian Broadcasting Corporation
and William Collins Pty Ltd, Sydney

This edition published in Great Britain in 1984

British Library Cataloguing in Publication Data
O'Reilly, Bill
The Bradman era
1. Bradman, *Sir* Donald
2. Cricket players – Australia – Biography
1. Title
796. 35'8'0924          GV915.B7
ISBN 0 00 218123 1

Typeset in Adelaide by Modgraphic Pty Ltd
Printed and bound in Great Britain by
Robert Hartnoll Ltd., Bodmin

## ACKNOWLEDGEMENTS

All photographs were taken from film supplied by the Cinesound
Movietone Film Library, with the exception of the following: outside
back cover*, 13*, 37*, 69*, 73*, 98/99*, 136*, 137*; Caroline Egan
5; *The Argus*, Melbourne 14/15; Herbert H Fishwick, by courtesy of
the *Sydney Morning Herald* 18, 19, 20, 21, 22, 23; Sport & General
Press Agency 25, 70, 71, 72, 77, 78, 83, 86, 87, 92, 93; courtesy of
MCC 75; Central Press 201.
* Every effort was made to identify and seek permission of the
copyright owner/s without success.

Designed by Howard Binns-McDonald
Edited by Helen Findlay and Nina Riemer

Cinesound Movietone Film Library photographs printed by Jon
Lewis and Phil Sheppard.
Statistics research – *England v Australia* by Ralph Barker & Irving
Rosenwater (Heinemann 1969), *Wisden Cricketers' Almanack* 1982, *And
Then Came Larwood* by Arthur Mailey (The Bodley Head 1933) and
*Australian Cricket – A History* by A G Moyes (Angus and Robertson 1959).

# INTRODUCTION

I have always loved old photographs.

In 1982 I started a television film project, with the general idea of making available a film and video cassettes of the cricket and cricketers of the past. When I found that it was practical to take stills from the original negative film, the book fell naturally into place.

Seeing all the old film for the first time in the process of transferring it onto video tape was an amazing journey backwards in time. The process of selecting individual frames and sequences—Grimmett cocking his wrist at the start of his delivery stride, Hammond at the point of impact with everything behind the shot's intended path, Bradman poised at the end of his follow through, watching the ball carve its way to the fence— was a unique lesson in techniques. There were some frustrations: Maurice Leyland wouldn't keep his head still; Keith Miller's body action was so quick that a movie camera couldn't stop it; and many a bowler disappeared behind the umpire at the point of delivery. Some of the photographs aren't perfect, but they aren't taking any more of them.

Bill O'Reilly's verbal style is as lively as his bowling, and has been left unchanged in the text, which is based on the narrative for the television film, complemented by much additional discussion and research, and many hours with the photographs, fitting them into the narrative and vice versa.

All but about thirty of the photographs are taken from the old film. Of the thirty, many of the team and group photographs were supplied from Bill O'Reilly's private archives, and the photographs of the 1928–29 series were taken by Herbert H Fishwick, who worked for the *Sydney Mail* and was one of the world's first great sports photographers.

It probably doesn't need to be spelled out, but the book is not intended to be a catalogue of every player of the 1930s and 1940s. I hope rather that it will give a feeling of what cricket was like in those days, and what it was like to be a Test cricketer.

My impression as an onlooker, after poring over hours of film and hundreds of photographs is, strangely, that Test cricket has not changed much.

They dressed differently off the field then. On the field, the game is only the sum of its parts, the players. Each cricketer is so different in style that unless basic techniques change radically, the game will always look much the same. I suspect that by the early 1930s, with Bradman, Hammond, Larwood and O'Reilly at the height of their powers, the technical aspects of style had been fully explored and exploited, and that the only really new factors which have entered the game since are the consistency which comes with more play and more practice, especially in the field, and the sheer natural athleticism of the West Indies.

I have no doubt that the elegance of a Chappell or a Gower would not have suffered in comparison with the Woolleys or Kippaxes of fifty years ago; Eddie Paynter has his present-day counterpart in Derek Randall; the venom of Jeff Thomson would have been as useful for Australia at Adelaide in January 1933 as the fire of Larwood would have been for England at Sydney in January 1983.

Whether or not the rising star of overs cricket will change techniques over a period to such an extent that Test cricket will look a different game, remains to be seen. My guess is that it will.

Those of us who no longer expect to be given, or to face, the new ball tend to forget the long hops and miscued square cuts of the past, preferring to recall the ball that pitched on middle and leg and took the off bail, the on drive that came right onto the meat and actually gathered pace as it approached the pickets. If cricket these days sometimes seems to be staggering from crisis to crisis and filled with unpleasant incidents, nothing the cricket world has seen could have been more unpleasant or created more of a crisis than the bodyline series in the 1930s.

But I expect that if I am around in fifty years I will look back on the cricket of the 1980s and say 'Yes, those were the days'.

There are many people without whom the project could not have been completed: Jim Whitbread of Cinesound Movietone Productions, who provided the film stock; John O'Reilly of ABC Sport and Glenn Hamilton and Howard Binns-McDonald of ABC Enterprises, whose enthusiasm kept it going; Albie Thoms, the producer of the television film, who knew how to get everything done; and Jon Lewis who printed the photographs from the old film with such care.

And finally of course, Bill O'Reilly, without whose knowledge, patience, and love of cricket . . . what can I say? I couldn't put it better than David Frith, editor of *Wisden Cricket Monthly* and one of the most knowledgeable cricket people around, who closed a recent letter to me as follows: 'I hear Bill O'Reilly is your narrator. I had many happy hours in his glorious company during the recent series. Give him my kindest when you see him'.

**Jack Egan**
**1983**

# HE WON'T DO WELL IN ENGLAND

Don Bradman was the greatest cricketer that I ever saw. In fact I'm certain that he was the best cricketer ever to walk onto a cricket ground in any part of the whole wide world.

I met him first in 1925, long before either one of us had ever been heard of in top class cricket.

Appropriately enough we met in the middle of a country cricket ground at Bowral, a mountain town about eighty miles south of Sydney. He was playing for Bowral, and I was representing a little town called Wingello, not far away.

He batted throughout the day, which was about four hours' play, and at the end of the day he had 234 not out, and I, with a very damaged reputation, looked forward to meeting him again on the following Saturday, when he resumed his innings.

The Gods of War smiled on me, I bowled him first ball of the day, so we finished that game with our honours even.

13

14

I went on to travel through first class cricket with him, practically from the first time ever that he played on the Sydney Cricket Ground. We played in the New South Wales Sheffield Shield side, and the first time I played in a Test with him was against the 1931–32 South Africans, when we won very easily. Then we played together in the Australian team during the 1930s, and later as a journalist I saw him right throughout the 1948 season in England.

The Australian XI *v* South Africa, fifth Test, Melbourne, 1932. *Standing* SJ McCabe, JH Fingleton, KE Rigg, WJ O'Reilly, H Ironmonger, LJ Nash, LS Darling *Seated* CV Grimmett, AF Kippax, WM Woodfall, DG Bradman, WA Oldfield

Bradman's batting talents were extraordinary. Firstly of course, he could see the ball, I think, quicker than any batsman ever to whom I bowled. As soon as the ball left your hand you could see him moving into the position where he reckoned he was going to make contact with the ball, and he would move aggressively and with tremendous speed.

His footwork was the best one could imagine. His strokemanship was comprehensive. His hooking was such that he could come down over the ball and hit it straight down to the ground at square leg, giving the infieldsmen no hope whatever of getting at it.

DG Bradman

His shots through the covers were beautifully timed, and always kept down on the ground. He could play an attacking shot savagely to any part of the field.

He loved to start his innings, first ball, with a push wide of mid on; that became almost his signature sign, but his tremendous array of attacking shots made him almost a frightening proposition for any bowler, despite any reputation that bowler might have.

And to cap it all off, it was part of Bradman's tremendous competitive spirit that he felt it his bounden duty to reduce every bowler to incompetency.

WR Hammond's cover drive. WA Oldfield the wicket-keeper.
Sydney Cricket Ground, 1928

Don Bradman played in his first Test at Brisbane against Percy Chapman's Englishmen in 1928. He failed there—he made 18 and 1, and he was dropped for the Sydney Test—but then he scored 79 and 112 in the third Test in Melbourne, and he made another century in the fifth Test, which was the only Test Australia won in that series.

The series was dominated by Walter Hammond, who made two centuries and two double centuries, and finished with 905 runs and an average of 113, but with Jack Hobbs, Herbert Sutcliffe, Douglas Jardine, Patsy Hendren, Harold Larwood and Maurice Tate, Chapman had one of the really great sides. They won the first four Tests, and no doubt they thought they would beat us pretty easily at home in England in 1930.

J Ryder tosses,
APF Chapman calls success-
fully.
First Test, Brisbane,
November 1928

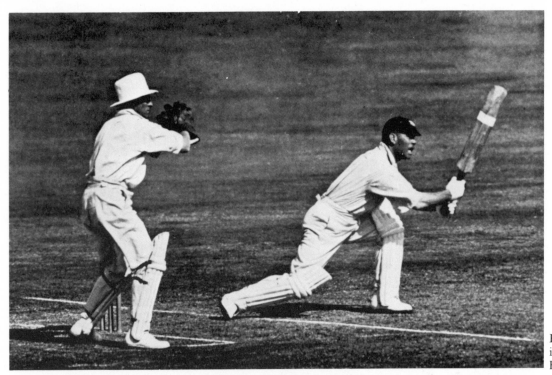

EH Hendren, during his
innings of 169.
First Test, Brisbane, 1928

APF Chapman caught (and
stumped) by Oldfield for 27
off Grimmett's bowling.
First Test, Brisbane, 1928

MW Tate bowling to
HS Hendry.
Second Test, Sydney, 1928

Harold Larwood bowling to
EL a'Beckett.
Third Test, Melbourne,
1928–29

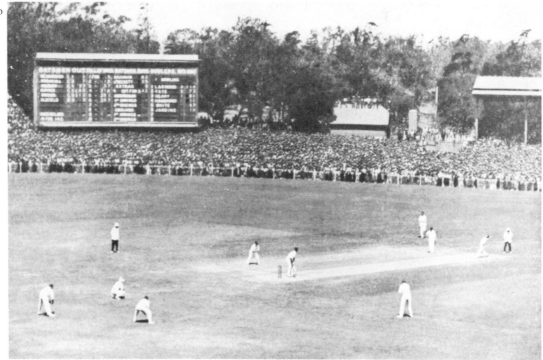

JB Hobbs driving
CV Grimmett. OE Nothling
at slip.
Second Test, Sydney, 1928

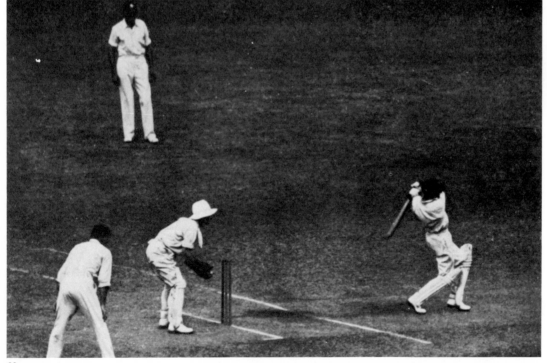

DG Bradman driving
JC White. Hammond at
slip, Geary forward of square
leg, Duckworth the
wicketkeeper.
Third Test, Melbourne,
1928–29

WM Woodfull caught Duckworth bowled Tate for 107. Chapman at gully, Hendren at short leg. Third Test, Melbourne, 1928–29

With those two centuries, Bradman had made his mark, but no one could have anticipated then what was to follow. In fact the Englishmen quickly observed that he often played cross-bat, and it was freely said, because of that, that he would have a lot of trouble on the English wickets.

# TOO GOOD
# TO LAST

As a twenty-one-year-old boy, Don Bradman went on his first tour to England in 1930, and there he scored a century in the first Test, a double century in the second Test, 334 in the third Test at Leeds—that was the world record score then—and another double century in the fifth Test at The Oval, where Australia won the series by two Tests to one.

He scored 974 Test runs in the series at an average of 139.14, a record which still stands and is likely to stand for a long time to come. Bradman himself says even now that the greatest innings he ever played was in the second Test at Lord's when he scored 254, and in that innings, he has often said, he did not hit one ball in the air throughout those 254 runs.

Bradman waves to the crowd after he had passed RE Foster's 287, previously the highest score in Tests. Third Test, Headingley, Leeds, July 1930

CV Grimmett bowling
during the first match of the
1930 tour, at Worcester

That was the last series for several of the really great English players: Chapman, who was captain in 1930; Frank Woolley, a tall, very graceful left-hander who made over three thousand runs in Tests; Jack Hobbs, probably as good a bat, with one exception, as ever there has been; and Maurice Tate, the medium pacer who took 155 Test wickets and was one of the game's great gentlemen. Maurice Tate came out to Australia in 1932–33, but he didn't play in a Test during that series.

APF Chapman facing PM Hornibrook. McCabe at slip, Richardson gully, Bradman mid-wicket. Second Test, Lord's, 1930

JB Hobbs and FE Woolley
opening for England.
Second Test, Lord's, 1930

FE Woolley about to pull a
ball from Grimmett.
Second Test, Lord's, 1930

That was a great tour for Clarrie Grimmett, too. He took 29 wickets in the Tests, and at Lord's, where he bowled 53 overs, almost half the overs in England's second innings, for the wickets of Hobbs, Woolley, Hammond and Hendren, as well as Gubby Allen and Maurice Tate, we probably could not have won without him.

In fact he got Hammond, who made all those runs in Australia in 1928–29, cheaply in both innings of the first two Tests and that was a great blow to England's hopes.

CV Grimmett

If any batsman got a hundred against a side that included Clarrie Grimmett among its bowlers, I wouldn't wait for any further proof that he was a top class batsman. Anyone who made a score against Grimmett was absolutely out of the top drawer, because if there was a weakness, in technique or temperament, he would bore away at it all day.

He was not a spectacular looking bowler: he had a short run and a flat trajectory, except when he was trying to cajole the tailenders out, but he could bowl all day on a plumb wicket at a pace and length which made it impossible for responsible batsmen to get down the wicket at him, and heaven help them if the pitch gave him any help.

That was the last tour for Archie Jackson, who also started in 1928–29 with a century in his first Test, and who was probably thought to be a more promising batsman than Don Bradman. He was a classical batsman, beautiful to watch, but he became ill on the 1930 tour, only played in one Test, and died of tuberculosis in 1933.

AA Jackson during his innings of 24 against Worcestershire. April 1930

But that series was completely dominated by Bradman's batting. Being so young, he gave the Englishmen a taste of what they were likely to get for the next twenty years.

Really, from an Australian point of view it was too good to be true, too good to last, and the bleak situation for the English bowlers was relieved a little bit in the last Test, the fifth Test at the Oval, where play went on on a rain-impaired pitch, and he seemed to flinch at one or two balls which got up round about shoulder high.

Bradman, at the start of his innings against Worcestershire, his first innings in England, where he made 236. April 1930

# SCONE THEORY

In the 1932–33 series the bodyline campaign mounted by the English attack under the command of Douglas Jardine presented to the cricket world the greatest crisis that ever it experienced.

Jardine had a very strong side. Hobbs had gone, but he still had Sutcliffe and Hammond, and he had Eddie Paynter and Maurice Leyland, two very good left-handers.

And he had four quickies—Harold Larwood, Gubby Allen, Bill Voce and Bill Bowes—and as soon as the team had been chosen, round about the end of August, those who had been to England in 1930 knew that there was some skulduggery going on, Douglas Jardine had something up his sleeve.

D R Jardine, 1932

35

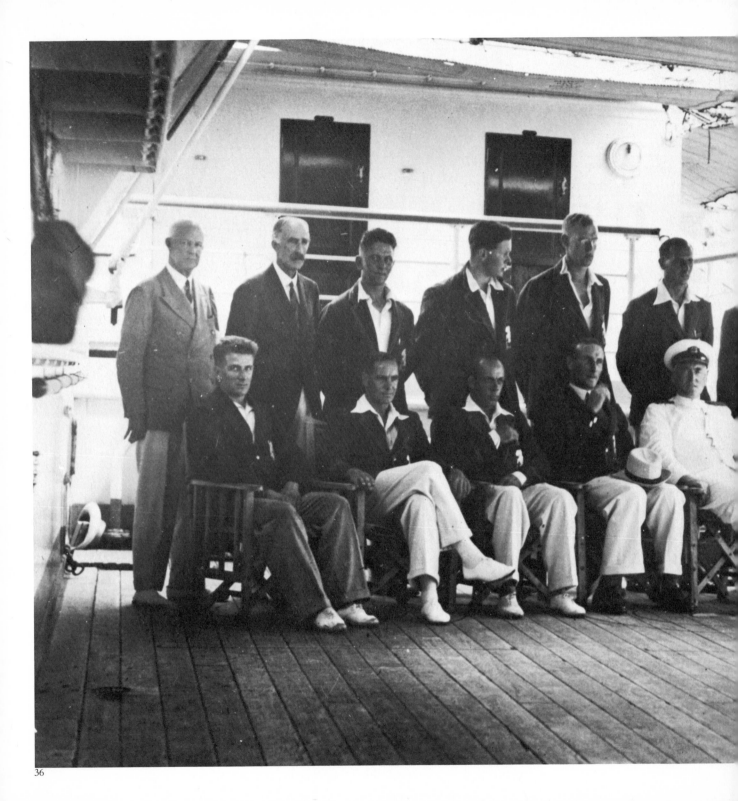

The English team of
1932–33 on board
RMS *Orontes*.
*Standing* PF Warner
(Manager), LCH Palairet
(Treasurer), M Leyland,
FR Brown, WE Bowes,
H Verity, W Voce,
E Paynter, Nawab of
Pataudi,
TB Mitchell *Seated*
H Larwood, H Sutcliffe,
RES Wyatt, DR Jardine,
Captain O'Sullivan,
GO Allen, WR Hammond,
G Duckworth, LEG Ames

DR Jardine in the nets,
WACA Ground, Perth,
October 1932

The tour started quietly enough. They had a draw against Western Australia, then they made some big scores: 583 for 7 wickets against a Combined Team which included Richardson, Fingleton, Bradman and McCabe, over 600 against South Australia, where they won very easily, and more than 400 against a strong Victorian team which had some good bowlers — Alexander, Nagel, Ironmonger, Fleetwood–Smith and Darling. They won that game by an innings too, with Hammond getting 200. Sutcliffe, Pataudi, Leyland and Jardine had also been in the runs.

Herbert Sutcliffe at the
Perth ground, 1932

LEG Ames and the Nawab
of Pataudi. Perth 1932

39

Then they came up against an Australian XI in Melbourne. England made 282 in their first innings, and the Australian XI made 218. Then in the second innings England collapsed for only 60, Lisle Nagel taking 8 for 32. Nagel was very tall, about six foot six, on the fast side of medium, and could float and seam the ball in the right conditions. The Englishmen had batted very slowly and not very well in the first innings, but in this innings Nagel really made them look silly, and I'm sure that this was in their minds when they came out to bowl in the Australian XI second innings.

They were only out there for a few overs, but they let us know in no uncertain terms what they were capable of. Allen bowled as fast as he could, which was very fast, but he never departed from the orthodox.

Larwood was a different matter. He was a magnificent bowler, of course, and he was at the height of his powers. He wasn't a tall man, but he was broad-shouldered and thick through the barrell—much the same build as Ray Lindwall, which is probably no coincidence. He had done well out here in 1928–29, and although he hadn't been able to stem the Bradman tide in England in 1930, back here on the hard wickets with his beautiful action, he could really make the ball fly.

Harold Larwood at the
Sydney Cricket Ground
during the 1932–33 series

*Overleaf:* Harold Larwood in
action

Bradman made 36 in the first innings of the Australian XI game, and in the second innings Larwood really turned it on for him. Now that was the first time that they'd really had a ping at him, and he made it clear that he wasn't going to let them hit him.

He still played his shots, but he took terrific risks, and you can see by the fact that he was bowled trying to cut a ball on the stumps that they had upset him, put him off his stride.

So that made their intentions clear, and when Bradman came back to Sydney I can remember him coming into the dressing room when we were playing somebody else, and he said that we were going to be Aunt Sallys, they were going to have a shot at us.

Leg theory has been a well-recognised bowling policy for years. The theory means that the bowler concentrates entirely on the leg stump and therefore of course the fieldsmen can be set in the various places to make run getting difficult.

Bodyline was totally different. Even a defensive shot was dangerous, because of the fieldsmen close in on the leg side.

You could step away to the off and try to hook, as Stan McCabe did so beautifully in the first Test, but that was dangerous too because of the chance of snicking a catch to the 'keeper, or being caught by the men out in the deep. And if you stepped away to leg to try to cut, well you ran the chance of being bowled.

Bradman bowled by
Larwood for 13. MCC *v* an
Australian XI, Melbourne,
November 1932

The point of leg theory was to keep the scoring rate down. It had been used in England since the early 1900s in county cricket, perhaps to force a draw, or perhaps in the hope that a batsman might get frustrated and play a rash shot.

What we saw in Australia in 1932–33 was something quite different, and really you could only say that the intention was to scare the daylights out of the batsman, and to put him right off his natural game. There was no doubt in our minds that when they put those five men close in on the leg side they were trying to hit the batsman, and Fingleton proved that when he took guard a foot outside leg stump, and still they bowled at him.

Douglas Jardine knew what had happened at the Oval in that last Test in 1930, and he knew that Bradman was the difference between the two teams. He decided to modify leg theory in his own way. The idea was to concentrate on the leg stump as usual, but to bowl the ball so short that it rose round about the shoulder and the head.

That is the reason why we Australians first called it the 'scone theory'. You'll know that in the Australian vernacular in the good old days the head was always referred to as 'the scone', and whenever a ball came up round about the head we used to call it a 'sconner'. In 1932–33 it was bowled so often that it became the 'scone theory'.

But later in the season a resourceful journalist, I think from Melbourne, hit upon the term 'bodyline'—bowling the 'body line'—and as a result that term has become famous, and it meant this: that the ball was bowled short, and a field was applied to it which made it impossible for a batsman to use his bat safely.

Five men were placed close in, almost as a leg slips field, and two on the boundary, and any batsman who decided to use his bat aggressively knew that he was taking his batting life in his hands.

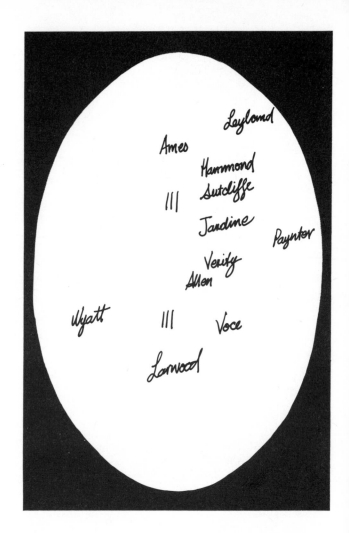

The full bodyline field employed for Larwood's bowling during the 1932–33 series

Bradman evading a bouncer
from Larwood

Facing bodyline, the batsman had several recourses. He could play the ball shoulder high in the middle of the bat, but one or two of the men were so close to him on the leg side that he ran the risk of the ball going to them on the full and being caught.

He could glance it, but then he had three men back in the leg slips position to take the catch.

He could hook it, which meant that he had to evade deep square leg, which was a very difficult proposition indeed, unless he was able to hit the ball straight down onto the ground, and not too many men have been able to do that on a ball shoulder high.

The batsman had one final alternative of course, if he wanted to score runs, and that was to move hurriedly away from the leg stump, away from the line of flight of the ball, and try to hit it past point or through the slips. And the final recourse was that he could just refuse to use his bat at all, he could just duck under it, and that's what most Australian batsmen did most of the time.

Bradman didn't, of course. He attacked it when he could, and he played some brilliant shots and some good innings, but he had to play recklessly, and so he wasn't a run-getting machine any more.

Stan McCabe attacked it too, but really they were the only two who were good enough to take it on with any chance of succeeding.

Don Bradman, due to illness, was unavailable to play in the first Test. We missed him completely there, of course, but fortunately for us Stan McCabe came to light with one of the epic innings of Test history.

There he scored 187 not out, and really he pulverised the English attack. McCabe when he was really going was a devastating hitter, and in that innings, as he did a few years later in South Africa, where Herbert Wade appealed against the light from the field because he was worried about his fieldsmen being injured, he completely demoralised the leg field.

He scored most of his runs in this innings from the pull and the hook, and later he was even going down the wicket and hitting Larwood wide of mid on. So then of course the close men on the leg side had to depart, and the whole bodyline theory fell to pieces.

Had we been lucky enough to have Bradman operating at the other end with McCabe, I'm certain that bodyline would have died its death then, long before we even started to talk about it as being bodyline.

McCabe hooking Larwood, during his innings of 187. Verity at short leg. First Test, Sydney, December 1932

Herbert Sutcliffe forces a full
toss from Wall past point
during the 1932–33 series

Australia's total was 360, then England made a very big score: Sutcliffe 194, and Hammond and Pataudi also made hundreds.

Herbert Sutcliffe typified the Yorkshire approach to cricket, and, in my view, he was the complete opener. He was a battler through and through, he had great pride in his ability to deal with any type of bowling in any conditions, and he would never let you know that you were causing him the slightest concern. If you beat him he would just throw his head back and look around the field as if he was deciding where he was going to put the next one.

So England finished up with 524. In the second innings we only made 164, and England only needed 1 run to win, so they won that Test quite handsomely.

| BATSMEN OUT. | | | FALL OF WKTS. | | BATSMEN. | RUNS. | BOWLERS. | WKTS | RUNS |
|---|---|---|---|---|---|---|---|---|---|
| SUTCLIFFE | B 3 | 33 | 1 FOR | 53 | | 4 | 1 WALL | 1 | 23 |
| LEYLAND | B 1 | 19 | 2 „ | 53 | BOWES | 2 | 2 IRONMONGER | 4 | 26 |
| PATAUDI | C 2 | 5 | 3 „ | 70 | EXTRAS | 5 | 3 O'REILLY | 5 | 66 |
| JARDINE | C 2 | 0 | 4 „ | 70 | 10 OUT FOR 139 | 4 GRIMMETT | | 19 |
| AMES | C 3 | 2 | 5 „ | 77 | AUSTRALIA | | 5 McCABE | | |
| HAMMOND | C 3 | 23 | 6 „ | 85 | 1ST INNINGS 228 | 6 BRADMAN | | |
| WYATT | LB 3 | 25 | 7 „ | 135 | 2ND INNINGS 191 | 7 O'BRIEN | | |
| ALLEN | S 2 | 23 | 8 „ | 137 | ENGLAND | | 8 RICHARDSON | | |
| VOCE | C 3 | 0 | 9 „ | 138 | 1ST INNINGS 169 | 9 FINGLETON | | |
| LARWOOD | C 2 | 4 | 10 „ | 139 | 2ND INNINGS | | 10 WOODFULL | | |

Scoreboard at the end of the
second Test, Melbourne,
January 1933

We went to Melbourne with a few changes in the Australian side with regard to our batting line up. Those two great players Alan Kippax and Bill Ponsford were dropped, and Don Bradman, back in the side, from the first ball he received in that series, went out to point and tried to hit Bill Bowes to deep fine leg. He connected all right, but only deflected it into his middle and leg stumps.

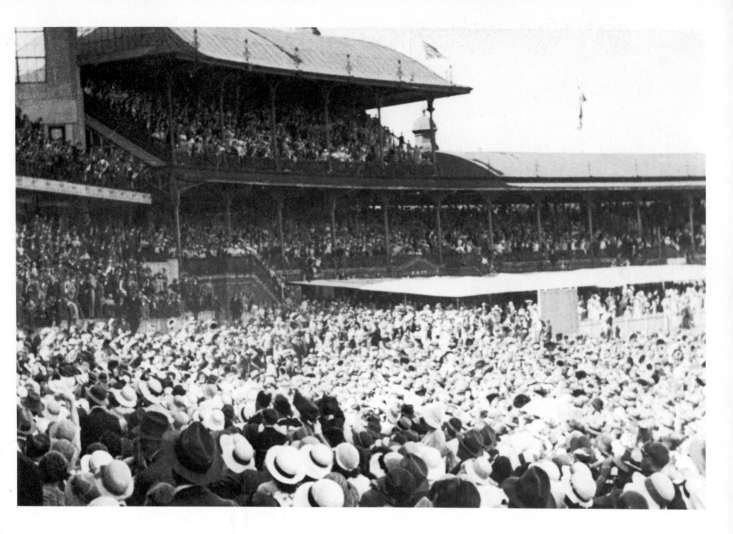

The crowd listening to the captains' speeches at the end of the Melbourne Test, 1933

That was a tremendous blow to us and to all the Australian aspirations for that series, and we only managed 228 in the first innings, due mainly to a fighting 83 from Jack Fingleton. Then Tim Wall and I got among the wickets and got England out for 169.

In our second innings Bradman made a beautiful century, a really good innings, 103 out of 191, and on a wearing pitch our spinners got England out for 139, so we went off to Adelaide for the third Test one all, and with our tails well in the air.

Woodfull struck over the
heart by Larwood early in
the Australian innings. In the
final photograph Allen tends
Woodfull, watched by
Jardine with hands on hips.
Bradman is the other
batsman.
Third Test, Adelaide,
January 1933

Crowd reactions in Adelaide were extraordinary. A big crowd came each day to the game, and they viewed this bodyline theory with great hostility, and they let us know right throughout the game how hostile they were towards it.

England batted first, we had them 4 for 30, but then Leyland, Wyatt, Paynter and Verity pulled them round and they totalled 341.

Soon after the Australian innings started Bill Woodfull was hit a terrific blow over the heart. Now when that happened, bodyline was not being bowled. He was hit by legitimate fast bowling, by a ball which ducked in quickly from Harold Larwood.

It was a tremendously painful blow and the crowd knew it — you would almost think that they felt it — but the thing that hurt them most, and it hurt me and all my team-mates too, was that when Woodfull had recovered sufficiently to take his bat up again and shape up, then the English bodyline field was set into operation, and everybody thought 'Hey . . . that's going just a little bit too far'.

We were in trouble early in the innings too, with Fingleton, Bradman and McCabe out for not many, Bradman and McCabe both being caught close in on the leg side.

Bradman caught Allen
bowled Larwood 8.
Third Test, Adelaide,
January 1933

Bill Ponsford was back in the side, he came in with padding from neck to knee, and he played a very game innings. He didn't like facing Larwood much, of course, none of us did, and it had been said that Larwood had his measure, but Ponny got on top of him in this innings, and he cut and drove whenever he got the chance, and Richardson and Oldfield backed him up well.

Then, just as it seemed as if Larwood was tiring and we might manage a reasonable score, Bert Oldfield was hit.

Strangely enough, bodyline was not being bowled then either. Bertie was batting very well indeed, and he went to hook a ball on about leg stump, and which was certainly not pitched short, but he hit it on the outside edge of his bat, and it ricocheted straight into his temple.

Oldfield collapsed and Woodfull came onto the field to take him off. He took no further part in the game.

WH Ponsford cuts Larwood high over the off side field during his innings of 85 in the Adelaide Test, 1933.

*Overleaf:* Oldfield is struck trying to hook Larwood. He collapses, and Woodfull comes onto the field to escort him off.
Third Test, Adelaide, January 1933

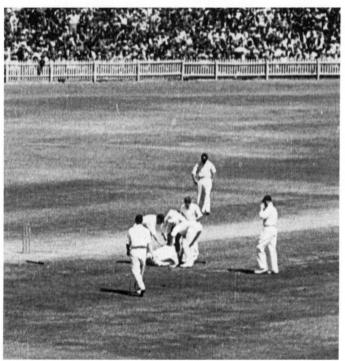

I was the next man in to bat, so I can give you first-hand information about the crowd. I reckon that it took me ten minutes to get in and to shape up to the first ball bowled to me by Harold Larwood. I wouldn't have minded if it had taken me twenty minutes.

The crowd just wouldn't sit down. They were roaring so loudly that Larwood, sitting on the ground way back in the distance, refused to bowl until they cooled down.

There were mounted troopers outside the fence who had instructions, I believe, to ride onto the ground if the crowd got out of hand.

I was bowled by Larwood for a duck, and we were all out for 222, the Englishmen made over 400 in the second innings and they won quite easily.

After Oldfield was hit, Woodfull spoke to Plum Warner, when Plum came into the Australian dressing room. Plum was the manager of the English team and he was one of the really big shots of English cricket. He came in to apologise to Woodfull for the hit that he'd got, and Woodfull had nothing more to say than:

'Look Plum, there are two teams out in the field there. One of them is playing cricket. The other is not.'

Plum, of course, left hurriedly. That to him was a tremendous insult. And then the pitch was set for the Australian Board of Control sending off their rather hostile cable, and a couple of days later came the English reply—so the whole situation then had blown up absolutely to fever heat.

18 January 1933

BODYLINE BOWLING HAS ASSUMED SUCH PROPORTIONS AS TO MENACE THE BEST
INTERESTS OF THE GAME MAKING PROTECTION OF THE BODY BY THE BATSMEN
THE MAIN CONSIDERATION STOP THIS IS CAUSING INTENSELY BITTER FEELING
BETWEEN THE PLAYERS AS WELL AS INJURY STOP IT IS OUR OPINION IT IS
UNSPORTSMANLIKE STOP UNLESS STOPPED AT ONCE IT IS LIKELY TO UPSET
THE FRIENDLY RELATIONS EXISTING BETWEEN AUSTRALIA AND ENGLAND STOP
AUSTRALIAN BOARD OF CONTROL.

The result of all that was that the feeling between the two teams, which had never been really good, then became completely hostile. An Australian considered it beneath his dignity to talk to an Englishman, and vice versa—they didn't like the idea of talking to us either.

There was very little fraternisation at all after the first Test match. The only man I can remember who would come and have a talk with us at any time—the only one probably that we were prepared to talk to—was Gubby Allen.

But when the MCC suggested that the tour be cut off there and then, wiser counsel prevailed. You can imagine how much they would have wanted to cut the tour off when they were creating record crowds at every ground, everyone wanting to be there to have a look at the fun that was going on out in the middle.

Remember this, no one in the Australian dressing room used the word 'bodyline' until about the fifth Test. When they started having a ping at us we'd say 'Hullo, the scone's on'.

When the 'scone theory' was being meted out there would have been no place conceivable that would have been more quiet than the Australian dressing room. We all sat around the windows looking out and the only time anyone would break the silence would be when one went extra close, and then you'd hear 'Oh 'struth, look at that one!'

And when a man would go out to bat you'd wish him the best and give him a smack on the back, almost with the feeling that you mightn't see him again on his feet — he might come back in on a stretcher.

Harold Larwood during the third Test, Adelaide, January 1933. The umpire is GA Hele.

McCabe has attempted a
defensive shot, but the ball
has been skied off the
shoulder of the bat. It fell
safely.
Fifth Test, Sydney, February
1933

We never really thought that the tour would be called
off. After Adelaide it cooled down a bit, and we went
on to play the fourth and fifth Tests, both of which
England won by several wickets.

But bodyline without doubt was the determining
factor of that series. It was designed to cut Bradman
down to size. It did that. His average was cut, from a
three figure average, down to the fifties.

That's what they set out to do in the first place, they
did it, and therefore away they went with the Ashes.

Bodyline was eventually banned. England saw a little of it from Larwood and Voce when they went home, and from the West Indies when they toured England later in 1933, and they realised that if it continued it would kill the game as we knew it.

Both countries got together in their legislative fields and they decided that it was to the best advantage of the game not to allow it to be played any longer.

They put it into the hands of the umpires under an intimidatory bowling piece of legislation, and from that time we've never had the slightest sign of bodyline in Test cricket.

We get bouncers nowadays of course, but bouncers and bodyline are as far apart as the poles, because of the restrictions on the field placings on the leg side and on the number of bouncers that can be bowled.

Bradman has moved across to the off in an attempt to glance Larwood, but is beaten by pace and bowled for 48 in the fifth Test in Sydney in 1933.

67

# THE PRODIGAL OF LEEDS

The bodyline series in 1932–33 was my first time ever against England, and my attitude was that I had very strong doubts whether there were any decent Englishmen in existence. It wasn't until I got to England in 1934 that I found out there were thousands upon thousands of them.

We went over there on the old SS *Orford*, and really that tour was an eye-opener as far as I was concerned.

We were invited to Windsor Castle as guests of the King and Queen, and Ramsay MacDonald, taking up the royal cue, invited us to Chequers, where Clarrie Grimmett gave him some cricket coaching.

During the first ten days, when we were in London before the cricket began, we had one or two functions every day, and if they were official you had to attend.

Bill O'Reilly and journalist
Ray Robinson on board
SS *Orford*, 1934

The 1934 Australians at
Windsor Castle.
*From left* CV Grimmett,
EH Bromley, WA Brown,
LS Darling, AF Kippax,
WH Ponsford, BA Barnett,
WC Bull (Treasurer),
WJ O'Reilly, WM Woodfull,
LO'B Fleetwood–Smith,
HM King George V,
AG Chipperfield, TW Wall,
HM Queen Mary,
H Bushby (Manager),
WA Oldfield, HI Ebeling,
SJ McCabe

Once the cricket began the number of functions was
reduced so they would not interfere too much with our
cricketing duties, but still everyone who owned a
theatre wanted the Australian cricket team to come
along, and if we did we would always get a wave from
the leading lady.

The camaraderie of those touring teams is something I know I am very lucky to have experienced: the leg-pulling, the baiting, the interminable discussions on the relative merits of Rugby and Australian Rules football, the constant teamwork and talk of tactics and the various ways to deal with our opponents on the field, many of whom became our good friends off the field, all these things served to build up friendships which have lasted the rest of our lives.

London 1934. Stan McCabe and Bill O'Reilly with Jim Foley, a Tasmanian-born businessman

The Australian touring team, 1934.
*Standing* WC Bull (Treasurer), AG Chipperfield, EH Bromley, WJ O'Reilly, H Bushby (Manager), HI Ebeling, TW Wall, LO'B Fleetwood-Smith, SJ McCabe, WF Ferguson (Scorer) *Seated* CV Grimmett, LS Darling, DG Bradman, WM Woodfull, AF Kippax, WH Ponsford, WA Brown *In front* BA Barnett, WA Oldfield

'Presented to Mr WJ O'Reilly with the compliments of Messrs Philips Lamps Limited as a souvenir of the visit of the Australian cricket team to the Philips Mitcham factory, England, August 16 1934'.

Of course there was a fair bit of hard work in it too. We played about thirty-five games on the tour, and we were often playing in pretty different conditions to what we were used to at home, and there was a lot of travelling involved, but we stayed in the top hotels and we were chauffeur-driven everywhere. None of us came from what you would call really well-off backgrounds, so we didn't find it hard to take, and of course everyone wanted to know us.

Then at the end of it there was another six weeks on the boat on the way back home.

For my part, I can thank cricket for having presented me with life-long friends like Len Darling, Stan McCabe, Leo O'Brien, Clarrie Grimmett, Hans Ebeling, Lindsay Hassett, Ernie McCormick and Jack Fingleton.

At the entrance gates to Chequers, Buckinghamshire, 1934.
H Bushby (Manager),
EH Bromley, BA Barnett,
SJ McCabe, TW Wall,
WJ O'Reilly, HI Ebeling

RES Wyatt and
WM Woodfull about to
toss. Wyatt won.
Fourth Test, Headingley,
Leeds, July 1934

In England in 1934 the Australian team was led by Bill Woodfull again.

As a batsman Woodfull was not spectacular. He had a very short backlift, there was no flourish, but he was a very good judge of a run and he was one of those batsmen that you would think was slow, until you looked up at the scoreboard.

WM Woodfull

As a captain he could foster tremendous loyalty in his players. There was not much outward sign of it, he was a very quiet man, didn't drink, smoke or swear, but he had a nice dry sense of humour, and out in the middle there was no sacrifice he was not prepared to make. He was a great model personally for any cricketer.

Woodfull and Ponsford
open the innings for
Australia.
First Test, Trent Bridge,
Nottingham, June 1934

We were absolutely determined to recover the Ashes of course, and at Trent Bridge, the first Test, we made 374 with good innings from Ponsford, McCabe and Chipperfield. England made 268, we got 273, Bill Brown 73 and McCabe 88, and then we bowled them out for only 141, so we won there, with only a few minutes to spare. In that game Clarrie Grimmett and I took nineteen of the twenty English wickets to fall.

But at Lord's it was Hedley Verity's game. England batted first and made 440, Cyril Walters 82 and Leyland and Ames a century apiece. Bill Brown got 105, but we only made 284, Verity 7 for 61, and in our second innings Verity took 8 wickets. We scored only 118, so we were beaten by an innings.

Wall caught Hendren bowled Verity for 1, to give Verity his fifteenth wicket, and England the second Test.
Lord's, June 1934
*From left* Hammond, Hendren, Umpire Hardstaff, Verity, Sutcliffe, O'Reilly, Geary, Wall, Ames

Second Test, Lord's,
June 1934.
The Australians are presented
to HM King George V.
*From left* SJ McCabe,
WA Brown, HI Ebeling,
DG Bradman, WA Oldfield,
AG Chipperfield,
AF Kippax, EH Bromley,
WJ O'Reilly, TW Wall,
LO'B Fleetwood-Smith,
HM King George V,
WH Ponsford, LS Darling,
CV Grimmett,
WM Woodfull, Lord
Cromer

HM King George V with
the English team.
Those visible *from left* Lord
Cromer, G Geary, H Verity,
WE Bowes, RES Wyatt,
M Leyland, EH Hendren,
Umpire J Hardstaff, Umpire
F Chester.
Lord's, June 1934

CF Walters off-drives
O'Reilly.
Third Test, Old Trafford,
Manchester, July 1934

In the third Test at Old Trafford Cyril Walters opened
with Herbert Sutcliffe. Walters never came out to
Australia, but in my view he was really a top liner. He
was a very polished player, he had all the shots, and he
was one English opener who was not afraid to use them.
When we came back after the 1934 tour I said Australia
was going to see an attacking opener out here in
1936–37, but he didn't come—I'm sure he would have
been picked but he was unavailable for family
reasons—and that season was the poorer for it, because
he would have done very well out here.

Wyatt bowled O'Reilly 0.
Third Test, Old Trafford,
July 1934

WR Hammond bowled
O'Reilly 4. Oldfield keeping
wicket, Wall at fine leg.
Third Test, Old Trafford,
July 1934

England made 68 in the first hour of the third Test, then after drinks—it was a very hot day—Darling caught Walters off me at short leg, I bowled Wyatt next ball, Hammond hit a 4, then I bowled him second ball.

M Leyland caught Barnett (sub.) bowled O'Reilly 153. *From left* Leyland, Oldfield, McCabe, O'Reilly, Barnett, Umpire Walden, Ames. Third Test, Old Trafford, July 1934

EH Hendren moves out to drive during his innings of 132.
Third Test, Old Trafford, July 1934

Patsy Hendren, who was forty-five years old then, came in next, and after Sutcliffe went, he and Maurice Leyland put on 191 for the fifth wicket.

Patsy was the most friendly opponent I ever bowled at. He was absolutely filled with good humour, he was always telling stories, and he would even tell them to you out in the middle.

He was a great believer in attack and getting right to the pitch of the ball, and he was always ready to lay on

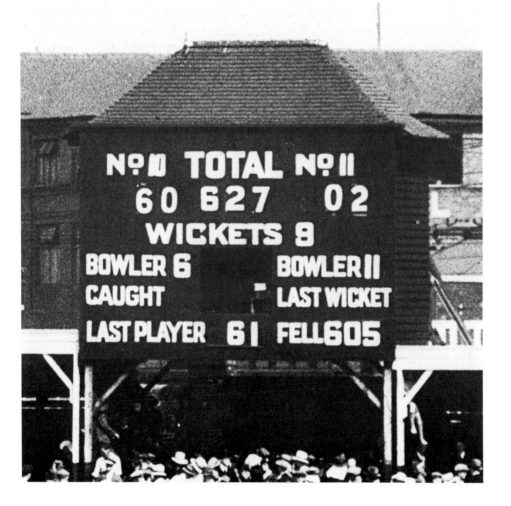

| | | | | | | |
|---|---|---|---|---|---|---|
| Nº **10** | | **TOTAL** | | **Nº 11** | | |
| **60** | | **627** | | **02** | | |
| | | **WICKETS 9** | | | | |
| **BOWLER 6** | | | | **BOWLER 11** | | |
| **CAUGHT** | | | | **LAST WICKET** | | |
| **LAST PLAYER 61** | | | | **FELL 605** | | |

The scoreboard at the declaration.
Third Test, Old Trafford,
July 1934

the power, particularly on the leg side. We always reckoned we had a chance of getting him early, especially as he got older, but once he was set he was a very tough customer to contain.

I eventually got Patsy, caught and bowled, and Leyland too, but not before they had made 132 and 153 respectively. I finished with 7 wickets, but England declared with 627 for 9.

We made 491, McCabe 137, but the game was eventually drawn.

Bradman hits a 4 off WE Bowes. This was the first ball he received in the fourth Test at Leeds. *From left* Verity, Bowes, Umpire Hardstaff, Hendren, Ponsford, Bradman, Hammond, Ames

We were terribly worried about Bradman throughout the early part of the tour, because he never played like the Bradman we knew. His feet just wouldn't work properly. His scores in the first three Tests were 29, 25, 36, 13 and 30, and he got out to the weirdest set of strokes ever I knew him to play.

We watched him go out at Leeds, the fourth Test: he got right behind the first ball from the fast bowler Bill Bowes, and he whacked it with terrific power wide of mid on, the very best shot I know in the game, and as

soon as he played it you could have heard the relief in the Australian dressing room, the cry of 'He's right! He's back!'

England had made only 200, and Bradman went in to join Ponsford on the first ball of the second day, when 3 wickets were down for 39. The next wicket fell a few minutes before stumps, when Ponsford trod on his wicket after making 181, and that partnership of 388 was a record for the fourth wicket.

Ponsford steers uppishly past Hammond at gully to bring up his hundred.
Fourth Test, Leeds, July 1934

87

A section of the crowd.
Fourth Test, Leeds, July 1934

Bradman went on to make 304, so in consecutive Test innings at Leeds in 1930 and 1934 he had made 638 runs. No wonder the crowds flocked to see him. But the significant thing from our point of view was that this innings marked Bradman's complete recovery from the bodyline campaign. That was all behind him now.

We finished with 584, then in England's second innings Hammond was run out, Walters, Hendren and Wyatt all got going, but we got them out, and

The end of the second day's play in the fourth Test at Leeds. Bradman, 271 not out, and McCabe, are escorted through the crowd

although Leyland batted well, at stumps on the fourth day they were still nearly 200 behind with only six wickets left, so we reckoned we had that game all sewn up, which would have put us one up in the series.

But it poured with rain that night, and again the next day, and the game was washed out with England still 150 behind, only four wickets standing. You can imagine how we felt.

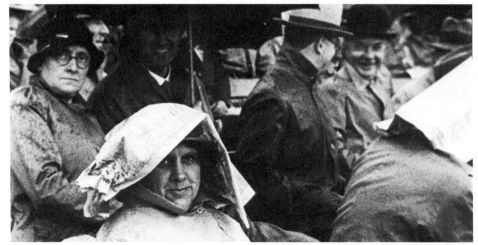

Headingley, Leeds, July 24, 1934

Australia batting during the fifth Test at the Oval, August 1934

At the Oval, we won the toss, Bradman joined Ponsford at 1 for 21, and again the partnership ended a few minutes before stumps on the same day, when Bradman was out for 244, Australia 472 for 2, and the record partnership of 451 for the second wicket still stands.

That was Bill Ponsford's last Test innings. He went on to make 266 which took him over the 2000 run mark in Tests, and he will always be remembered for his prolific scoring—he made over 400 in an innings twice.

Australia's total was 701, and we won the game by over 500 runs, so we came home with the Ashes.

WM Woodfull square cuts Verity.
*From left* Woolley (keeping wicket following an injury to Ames), Hammond, Clark, Woodfull, Umpire Chester, Wyatt, Verity, Ponsford, Walters, Allen, Umpire Walden.
Fifth Test, The Oval, 1934

DG Bradman
Second Test, Lord's, June
1934

# THE LUCK OF THE TOSS

In 1935–36 Australia went to South Africa. Bradman didn't go on that tour: he had been very ill after the 1934 tour in England, had come back late, and then had moved from New South Wales to live in South Australia. Victor Richardson captained that side, and we won the series four to nil, with one Test drawn.

Then in 1936 England under the captaincy of Gubby Allen came to Australia, and Australia was captained by Don Bradman himself.

Gubby Allen was a forthright, knowledgeable cricketer, and certainly one of cricket's most respected figures. Everybody had a soft spot for Gubby.

He was a good fast bowler, if not one of the greats, and he was an enormous trier—he used to get very upset if he didn't perform up to his own expectations, and he was the first bowler I ever heard cursing himself out loud if he sent down a short one or a wide. He was a very useful bat too, and an outstanding field close to the wicket, and later on he did a great job as President of the MCC for many years.

DG Bradman about to toss.
GO Allen calls correctly.
First Test, Brisbane,
December 1936

The 1935–36 Australian
touring party in rickshaws at
the Royal Hotel, Durban,
South Africa.
WF Ferguson (Scorer),
WA Oldfield, WJ O'Reilly,
LPJ O'Brien, JH Fingleton,
WA Brown, SJ McCabe,
VY Richardson, LS Darling,
EL McCormick, MW Sievers,
AG Chipperfield,
BA Barnett, CV Grimmett,
WF Lamprecht (South
African Manager), H Rowe
(Manager)

The Paddington Hill and 'bob' stand during the second Test, Sydney Cricket Ground, December 1936

England batted first in Brisbane and made 358, Leyland 126. Fingleton made 100 exactly in our first innings of 234, England replied with 256, and then we were caught on a wet wicket and were all out for 58 in our second innings.

Then in Sydney, Allen again won the toss. In those days if you won the toss you batted—never a thought of anything else—if you look at the records you'll see that every side winning the toss batted first. Walter Hammond came back to his best form with 231 and England were 426 for 6 when rain came. They declared, and after being 3 for 1, O'Brien, Bradman and McCabe

| BOWLER | WKTS | RUNS | | | BATSMEN | OUT | FoⁿW |
|---|---|---|---|---|---|---|---|
| BARNETT | | | | | O'BRIEN | 0 | 1 |
| FAGG | | | ENGLAND 426 | | BRADMAN | 0 | 1 |
| HARDSTAFF | | | | | M°CABE | 0 | 1 |
| LEYLAND | | | | | | | |
| ROBINS | | | | | | | |
| SIMS | | | | | | | |
| HAMMOND | | | BATSMEN | | | | |
| VERITY | | | FINGLETON | | | | |
| VOCE | 3 | 1 | CHIPPERFIELD | | | | |
| ALLEN | | | 3 FOR 1 | | SUNDRIES | | |

BAR

back in the pavilion, we scrambled to 80. In our second innings we topped 300 with Fingleton, Bradman and McCabe getting the runs, but we still lost by an innings.

An extraordinary thing happened to me in that first innings in the Sydney Test: there I had the experience of becoming top scorer for Australia. I was still unconquered, 37 not out, when I ran out of batting partners, and I lodged a complaint immediately with my captain when I got to the dressing room, to tell him that I wanted to be tried further up the list next time.

Scoreboard early in the Australian innings. Second Test, Sydney, December 1936

WJ O'Reilly, first Test,
Brisbane, December 1936.
J Hardstaff backing up.
The umpire is G Borwick

With my bowling, my cardinal rule was that I always had my eyes glued on the spot where I was going to pitch the ball. I wasn't a slow leg spinner, I bowled medium pace. The leg spinner was my stock ball, but I bowled the wrong'un more frequently than any other leg spinner I've seen. It was nothing for me to bowl it three times in an eight ball over: I had complete confidence in my ability to bowl a wrong'un to length and direction, and I could really get it to bounce, so I used it as a variation of flight and bounce as well as spin.

When I started I used to bowl the orthodox off break, but I gave that up because it interfered with my rhythm, but my straight faster ball got me a lot of wickets—I even had a bouncer of sorts, and I took Keith Rigg's cap off with it once.

Clarrie Grimmett, to my great consternation, was not picked to play for Australia in that 1936–37 series, even though he had taken 44 wickets in South Africa at less

than 15 apiece. His place was eventually taken by Fleetwood-Smith, who had his first Test in Melbourne, the Third Test. Fleetwood-Smith was a left arm wrist spinner, and he could spin the ball prodigiously either way. If he was not one of the great cricket brains, he had, I think, more natural ability than any other spin bowler I ever saw. But for the rest of my career, I always missed having Grimmett down the other end.

GO Allen caught McCabe
bowled O'Reilly for 35.
First Test, Brisbane,
December 1936

The Members' Stand at the
Melbourne Cricket Ground,
taken from the Press box

So we arrived in Melbourne for the third Test of that
1936–37 series two down, three to play. Bradman had
had two tests as captain and we had lost them both, and
no doubt his captaincy came under some suspicion.
There was an element of tremendous doubt about
whether he could lead the side successfully.

He very quickly put that to rest when he won the three
tosses in the remaining Tests. He made two double
centuries and a century himself, and we kept the Ashes
by winning the last three Tests.

In Melbourne we made 200. England had their turn on
a wet wicket and collapsed for 76, then in the second

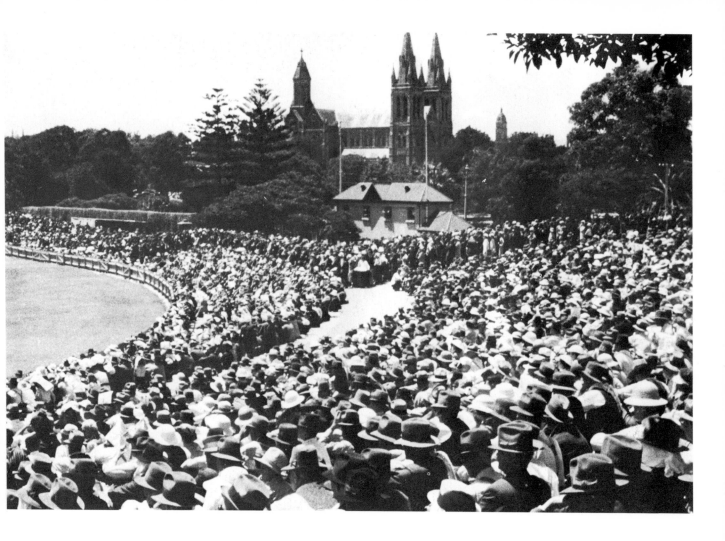

Adelaide Oval, January 1937

innings, the wicket still dangerous, I got my wish: Leslie
O'Brien Fleetwood–Smith and I were asked to open the
batting for Australia. I was out first ball for a duck,
Fleetwood–Smith faced twenty-six deliveries before he
got bat to ball. He hit the twenty-seventh, and it was
caught by Verity, so he was out for nothing too.

Later, after the wicket had settled down, Jack
Fingleton, 136, and Bradman, 270, put on 346 for the
sixth wicket, another Test record which still stands. We
made 564 and won by over 300 runs.

K Farnes in action during the fifth Test, Melbourne, February 1937. He took 6 for 96

Adelaide was a closer game. England led by 40 on the first innings, and although we made over 400 in the second innings, Bradman 212, on the last day England needed 244 with 7 wickets in hand, Hammond still in.

Fleetwood-Smith put the issue beyond doubt in his first over of the day, when he bowled Hammond with a perfectly pitched wrong'un which spun a yard, and he went on to take 6 wickets in the innings and 10 wickets for the match. The series was all square with one Test to play.

In the final Test, back in Melbourne, the English fast
bowler Ken Farnes took 6 wickets, but Bradman and
McCabe put on 250 for the third wicket, then when
they were out Jackie Badcock and Ross Gregory put on
another 150 for the fifth wicket, so we made 604. Again
the weather took a hand, this time to England's
disadvantage, and they were out fairly cheaply twice, so
we kept the Ashes. Really, we'd come back from the
dead, and because the series was so close we had huge
crowds and cricket was back on top of the world.

# ENGLISH REVIVAL

Back in England in 1938, under the captaincy of Don Bradman, we met England led by Walter Hammond, who had turned from professionalism to become an amateur so he could captain his country.

Hammond was a good, safe captain. He did nothing unpredictable, and, like Bradman, he was struck with the wand of genius, so he had the advantage of being able to win a game off his own bat.

He was also a very useful change bowler, economical and analytical, capable of thinking a good batsman out, and he was a wonderful slip field, able to catch practically anything with extraordinary ease and grace.

At Trent Bridge, the first Test, we saw three young Englishmen for the first time. They were the opening batsman, a very correct player, Len Hutton, a less orthodox but equally brilliant batsman, Denis Compton—both of them made centuries against us in this Test—and a very energetic young all-rounder, Bill Edrich. He didn't do much in this series, but his career blossomed later on.

W R Hammond, 1938

111

*From top* L Hutton, DCS Compton, and WJ Edrich. 1938

Trent Bridge pavilion, June 1938

The pavilion at Trent Bridge was a beautiful old building, but most of the English grounds are all much smaller than ours out here, and so far as I was concerned that just made it a lot easier for the batsman.

They were second class too, in my day anyway, so far as players' accommodation was concerned: showers were pretty hard to find and communal baths were not what we were used to.

Some of the grounds were quite beautiful, of course: Chesterfield, Derbyshire, Worcester, Fenners at Cambridge; but the ovals where we played the Tests were mostly in industrial areas, and I was never really taken with them.

Play in progress during the first Test, Trent Bridge, June 1938

The crowds in England were very much more reserved than ours, except in Yorkshire, where they really knew their cricket and weren't backward in letting us know what they thought. But it was only there that we ever saw anything resembling a good throaty Melbourne crowd.

In the South they didn't seem to have the same knowledge of the game, so far as I could judge from the middle, and they were terribly quiet. A man felt that by appealing too loudly you might be interrupting the pleasantness of the day.

Crowd scenes during the
first Test at Trent Bridge,
1938

CJ Barnett and L Hutton
open the innings for
England.
First Test, Trent Bridge,
1938

Barnett and Hutton, in his first Test, opened for England at Trent Bridge, and very early on Hutton played onto his stumps, but the bail didn't come off— the same thing that happened to me with Herbert Sutcliffe in the first Test of the 1932–33 series. They both made hundreds, Compton got his century too, and Eddie Paynter, that grand little jumping-jack of a cricketer, made 216.

Australia's openers in the first Test, JH Fingleton and WA Brown

Hammond declared at 8 for 658, and at stumps on the second day we were not much more than a hundred, Fingleton, Brown and Bradman out, and the situation for us looked hopeless. We were 500 behind with only 7 wickets left, three days to play.

Then we saw one of the really great Test innings.

Stan McCabe had become an immortal with his 187 in Sydney in 1932. He played another great innings in Johannesburg in 1935, and here at Nottingham, with his 232, he summed his whole career up, as if to show the world for ever what a great player he was.

SJ McCabe back cuts during
his innings of 232.
First Test, Trent Bridge,
June 1938

I would say that McCabe was the best hooker I ever saw, and his cutting, where he transferred his weight from the front foot to the back foot as he made contact, was an absolute picture to see.

There's no doubt, anyone who saw him at his top, and I saw each of those three great innings, would class him as one of the most spectacular batsmen ever.

At one stage we were 6 for 194, and after the seventh wicket fell at 263 Stan McCabe made 127 runs out of 148, in eighty minutes. We had to follow on, but Brown and Bradman made a century each, and we saved that game.

Lord's pavilion, June 1938

At Lord's, we had another draw, but we saw two more great innings. Hammond's 240 in England's first innings of 494, and Bill Brown, who carried his bat for 206 in the Australian innings of 422.

Hedley Verity took 4 wickets, including Bradman, in the first innings of this Lord's Test, and we were a bit worried that he might run through us again in the second innings as he had done here at Lord's in 1934, where he had taken 15 wickets.

But Bradman batted in his very best form for 102 not out, Linday Hassett supported him well, and at the end we were 111 runs short with 4 wickets still in hand.

The Australian team is presented to HM King George VI.
Those visible, *from left* are: Stanley Baldwin, SJ McCabe, BA Barnett, JH Fingleton, EL McCormick, DG Bradman, WJ O'Reilly, HM King George VI, AG Chipperfield, CL Badcock, AL Hassett, MG Waite, SG Barnes. Second Test, Lord's, June 1938

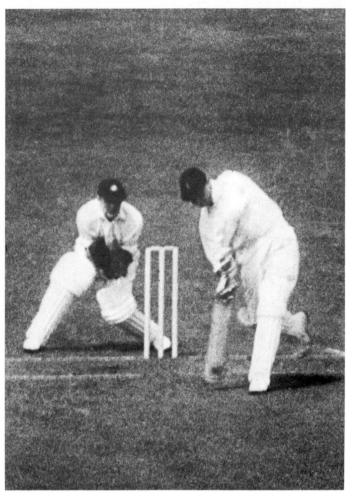

Walter Hammond's cover
drive, 1938. The wicket-
keeper is BA Barnett

This Lord's Test was Walter Hammond's last big innings against Australia. Hammond was a tremendously vigorous strokemaker, and once you had seen him bat, if you knew your cricket, you would never forget it.

He was always very keen to get to the pitch of the ball—I have seen him go down eight or ten feet to get at Clarrie Grimmett—and he was a truly phenomenal cover driver, the best I have seen for the sheer perfection of execution of that stroke.

It was said that he had a weakness on the leg side, but that was not my experience. He didn't hook, and he lacked shots behind square leg, but he was an effective accumulator of runs on the leg side, although his shots there paled in comparison with his off side play.

WA Brown turns Farnes to
leg for a single during his
innings of 206 not out in the
second Test at Lord's in 1938

There was no doubt about the fact that Bill Brown's unbeaten double century in the Lord's Test saved that game for us.

He was a meticulously careful player who delighted in making every shot look as good as he possibly could. You would almost think that he had practised his strokes in front of a mirror: in fact the English used to regard him as a model for his dress, stance, stroke execution and follow through.

He had a good opening bat's outlook—he gave nothing away at all, never took risks or indulged himself—and although early in his career he had very few shots, he developed them as he went along, and he became a very natty batsman. A hundred from Bill Brown might take a while, but it would be a very pleasant affair.

Hedley Verity, who with Ken Farnes, another member of this 1938 English side, was to die in World War II, was a fine bowler. So he should have been, because he was a protégé of Wilfred Rhodes, one of the all-time greats, and Rhodes took him under his wing when he was a youngster and always took a keen interest in him.

He was just over six feet tall, strong and very athletically built. He was very accurate, just a bit quicker than slow, and with a good amount of spin.

He had a real Yorkshireman's outlook, played it hard all the time, and another thing I remember about him, he had the quietest appeal I ever heard: he was always at the umpire, he might appeal once an over, but always very quietly.

Hedley Verity during the second Test at Lord's in 1938. McCabe is backing up, Umpire Walden is at the bowler's end, and Farnes is at mid off.

The Leeds Test was an exciting affair too. The wicket was damp, England made 223, Hammond 76. Then, in bad light most of the time, Bradman scored 103 out of 242. The conditions were ideal for spin bowling, Fleetwood-Smith took 4 wickets, I got 5, and England only made 123. So we only needed 105 to win, but we were 4 for 61 before Lindsay Hassett made the game safe with some sensible hitting.

The Manchester Test was washed out, not a ball bowled, so we went to the Oval one up and the best England could do was to square the Ashes.

DG Bradman's celebrated pull shot. WFF Price is the wicket-keeper.
Third Test, Leeds, July 1938

Bradman has called
incorrectly, watched by
Hammond and ground
manager 'Bosser' Martin.
Final Test, The Oval,
August 1938

This Test was made famous by the world record score
by Leonard Hutton from Yorkshire, who made 364.
He broke Bradman's record which had stood since
1930, and in fact he still holds the record for England
against Australia.

Hammond won the toss, and it was a good one to win, because the wicket was absolutely as dry as a bone.

England's first wicket fell at 29, Hutton was joined by Maurice Leyland, who was out, run out, some time the next morning for 187, England 2 for 411.

The heavy roller in use at The Oval, under the supervision of 'Bosser' Martin.
Final Test, 1938

Maurice Leyland brings up
a cloud of dust, and 4 runs,
during his innings of 187 in
the last Test of the 1938
series

Eddie Paynter drives, but fails to score. The wicket-keeper is BA Barnett, F Walden is the umpire. Final Test, the Oval, 1938

Maurice Leyland and Eddie Paynter were the two great English left-handers of the 1930s and, being a leg spinner, I took a special interest in them.

Leyland was a dry, likeable Yorkshireman, everybody liked him, and he had a very adventurous outlook—if the ball was up to him he would hit it every time. The problem was how to make him think it was up when it wasn't. My stock ball was on his off stump coming in, and he often used to just cover up, so I used the wrong'un a lot to him. He made plenty of runs off me, but I got him ten times in Tests: he and Walter Hammond, who I got eleven times, were my most frequent Test wickets.

Eddie Paynter was only pint sized—he could have been a jockey—but he was a very aggressive, busy little player. He had one unique shot against the fast bowlers: he would jump up in the air and spin round to flick them round the corner.

131

After Leyland went, Hammond came in and made 59, but we got him out, and we got Eddie Paynter for 0 and Denis Compton for 1. But then Hardstaff came in and he eventually made 169. Hutton just went on and on; at stumps on the second day England were 5 for 634. Hutton had been there for two days and he was 300 exactly, I remember. He went on to get his 364, it took him over thirteen hours, and England closed at 903 for 7 wickets.

Fleetwood-Smith bowled 87 overs, I bowled 85, Mervyn Waite bowled 72 and Stan McCabe and Siddy Barnes bowled 38 overs each. Even Bradman had a bowl, but he twisted his ankle in the process and couldn't bat. Fingleton was injured in the field too, and we made 201 in our first innings and 123 in our second.

LO'B Fleetwood-Smith delivering one of the 522 balls bowled by him during the Oval Test, 1938. His analysis was 87.11.298.1

Len Hutton takes a single to square leg to reach a century, and acknowledges the crowd's applause, during his record innings of 364 in the Oval Test, 1938. The final photograph includes SG Barnes, patting Hutton on the back, and Umpire Frank Chester.

So England won that final Test very easily, but the series was tied at one Test each, and we held onto the Ashes. England, with their new players, was looking to be a formidable side again. It was our turn to look for new blood.

McCabe, Fleetwood-Smith, O'Reilly and Hassett with a group of admirers during the 1938 tour

That Test at the Oval, where Len Hutton got his record, was my last Test in England, and I'd have to say that it wasn't a game I enjoyed much, but it would have done English cricket a lot of good if war hadn't come.

At the Nottingham War Memorial gates, June 1938. *From left* WA Brown, SG Barnes, EL McCormick, BA Barnett, WH Jeanes (Manager), DG Bradman, MG Waite, LO'B Fleetwood-Smith, AL Hassett, AG Chipperfield, SJ McCabe, CW Walker, WJ O'Reilly, ECS White, FA Ward, JH Fingleton, CL Badcock

# NEW FACES

After the Second World War finished, we saw Australia facing up to England, in Australia, against Walter Hammond's 1946–47 side.

Bradman was again the captain, and the Australian team appeared to be absolutely a team of young hopefuls, mostly unheard of, but some of them of course by now have become Australian heroes.

For instance, Siddy Barnes, Keith Miller, Arthur Morris, Ernie Toshack, Neil Harvey, Don Tallon, Ray Lindwall, Bill Johnston, Ian Johnson. Those names became household names, but in 1946 they all had to make their reputations, except perhaps Sid Barnes, who had played in the final Test in 1938, and Keith Miller, who had gone a long way towards making his reputation with the Services XI in England just after the war.

AR Morris     ERH Toshack

IW Johnson     SG Barnes

Keith Miller was the greatest all-rounder of his time, and perhaps the most talented individual ever to step onto a cricket ground—you would have to bracket him with Gary Sobers in that category.

He was always an absolutely dynamic personality on the field, and he had more followers around the world than anyone in the game bar Bradman.

The first time I saw him I realised his potential as a batsman. I was playing against him, and he hit one of the best hundreds I ever saw. I used to encourage him to give bowling away, because in my view his batting was never fully developed. He was such a good bowler too, and did so much bowling, that his batting suffered.

He didn't hook, but he played every other shot with the most complete ball sense and athleticism.

KR Miller square cuts. 1947

Miller was a tremendously destructive and unpredictable new ball bowler: he could get terrific lift and pace from the pitch, but he was just as likely to bowl a leg break in the middle of the first over.

As a fieldsman he was also completely inspired. I've seen him take the most extraordinary catches, where you never even thought about it being a catch until Miller picked himself up off the ground and tossed his hair back out of his eyes. Then you'd see he had the ball in his hand.

So he could win a game in any department. In my view he was the ideal cricketer, and he did an enormous amount of good for the game because he was such a good advertisement for it.

K R Miller 1947

RR Lindwall 1947

Ray Lindwall I saw right from the time he was in short pants. When he first came into the St George side in Sydney grade cricket I was his captain, then I played with him in the New South Wales side, and also when he first came into the Australian side, when we had a short tour to New Zealand in 1946.

He was a very thoughtful, rather shy boy, who regarded fast bowling as a wonderful outlet for his personality. He was also an accomplished Rugby League player, and could have had a career there if he had wanted it.

He had every weapon in the fast bowler's armoury: genuine pace, control, he was always thinking about how to get the batsman out, and he could swing the ball late, either way.

At last we had a truly great fast bowler—a bowler to compare with Harold Larwood, and if you asked me to name which was the greatest, I'd say add one name, Denis Lillee, and you could take your pick. The three of them would rate equally in my book.

With Ray Lindwall and Keith Miller, Don Bradman was lucky to have at his disposal one of the really great fast bowling combinations.

Bradman cutting Lindwall.
Barnes at short leg, Saggers
the wicket-keeper.
Testimonial match,
Melbourne, 1948

The Bradman after the war was of course not comparable with the young athlete who scored all those runs back in 1930 and later in 1934 in England.

He had lost a lot of his speed afoot and his aggression had dropped quite a lot. But with those few disparaging remarks, I tell you that he was still the best batsman in the world.

He had always been an old head on young shoulders. The shoulders weren't so young now, but the cricket brain was as good as ever, the determination to succeed hadn't diminished, and of course his footwork was so good, he got into position so well, that so long as he could still see the ball, well you could back him to score a hundred as often as not.

PA Gibb and TG Evans in the nets at Perth at the start of the 1946–47 MCC tour

England, with Compton, Hutton, Edrich, Wright, and new men like Bedser, Evans and Washbrook, had some very good players, but Voce was getting on in years, and Edrich, although he was useful and a great trier, just lacked that innate ability which makes a great bowler, although he had a good tour with the bat.

And Hammond, too, didn't have a successful series, or a happy tour. I've always thought it a great shame that a new generation of cricket followers out here in 1946–47 saw only the shadow of a great cricketer, because Walter Hammond made over 7000 runs in Tests, and he really was one of the top batsmen of cricket history.

Rupert Howard, manager, and Walter Hammond, captain, during the 1946–47 MCC tour

AV Bedser

Alec Bedser was a great bowler, but he never really had a partner worthy of him. They say great fast bowlers come in pairs, and it doesn't just apply to fast bowlers — any bowler finds that if the man at the other end isn't putting pressure on the batsman, then it makes his job that much harder, and I'm sure Bedser suffered from that out here in 1946–47, and probably right throughout his career.

Bedser worked first of all on the absolute fundamentals: length and direction. He kept up a good line and length all the while. Then, with those essentials in mind, what made him a difficult proposition for any batsman, even Bradman, was his ability to move the ball each way off the pitch.

When the wicket gave him any help at all he was a very dangerous bowler, because he was always on line, the batsman had to play at him all the time, and if the ball was seaming, just short of a length, there was a very good chance of it catching the edge.

DVP Wright

Doug Wright had the most potential of any leg spinner who played for England in my time. He was a similar bowler to me, he bowled close to medium pace, had a wrong'un, and could make the ball lift.

In England in 1938 we thought he was the best bowler in the English side, and we always thought that he didn't get enough encouragement from the powers that be at home, where wrist spinners have never been fashionable.

Apart from that he did have a continuing difficulty
with his run. He had a very bouncy, hoppy approach
and he often had trouble finding a good rhythm, and
sometimes bowled short as a result.

  He was a very quiet, gentlemanly cove, who knew the
game thoroughly. I heard that later on he was teaching
cricket at a school in Kent, and they were lucky boys to
have Doug Wright coaching them.

The Hill and the Sheridan
Stand. Sydney Cricket
Ground, 1946

England were unlucky in Brisbane, where Australia
made 645, Bradman 187 and Hassett 128, and then a
thunderstorm produced a sticky wicket for England
and they were out cheaply twice.

Then they came down to Sydney for the second Test.
The Sydney Cricket Ground is generally regarded by
cricketers, certainly by Australians, as the best cricket
ground in the world. Taking the weather and the light,
the pitch, the general setting and playing conditions
into consideration, I would say it deserves that ranking,
although my best performances were at Melbourne.
That was my favourite ground.

The Old Members' Stand
and the Ladies' Stand, from
the MA Noble Stand.
Sydney Cricket Ground,
1947

Bradman and Hassett lead the
Australian team onto the
Sydney Cricket Ground,
followed by Toshack.
Second Test, December 1946

Sydney Cricket Ground, second Test *v* England, December 1946

On the Paddington Hill

The bar under the scoreboard on the Hill

The Ladies' Stand

View from the sightscreen at the Randwick end

Arthur Gilligan

George Duckworth

I was in the Press box for this series, and I was in illustrious company. The team we had up there was as good as either of the two sides out on the field.

At this Sydney Test there was Warwick Armstrong, 'Stork' Hendry, Bill Woodfull, Jack Fingleton, Victor Richardson, Alan Kippax, Stan McCabe, Bill Bowes, George Duckworth, Arthur Gilligan and Clarrie Grimmett, which isn't a bad eleven. There were plenty of other cricketers too, as well as the professional journalists like Neville Cardus, EM Wellings and EW Swanton.

Alan McGilvray

Arthur Mailey

Hammond won the toss in Sydney. Lindwall was unavailable, Miller had Hutton in all sorts of trouble early on, but it was the spinners who took the wickets.

Hutton made 39, Ikin 60, and Edrich top scored with 71, but it was a good wicket, and really the English batsmen could have made a lot more, but they just wouldn't use their feet to the slow bowlers. Ian Johnson took 6 wickets and McCool got Edrich, Compton and Hammond.

Len Hutton troubled by a
bouncer from Miller.
McCool at first slip, Johnson
at second.
Second Test, Sydney,
December 1946

WJ Edrich drives GE Tribe
through mid on for 4 during
his innings of 71.
Second Test, Sydney, 1946

TPB Smith lbw to Johnson
without offering a shot.
*From left* Johnson,
Umpire Borwick, Miller,
Ikin, Smith, Tallon, Barnes,
McCool, Hassett
Second Test, Sydney, 1946

Ian Johnson was the rule-of-thumb type of off spinner—I would call him a looper—he gave the ball plenty of air, and he got quite a bit of turn.

He had a good, aggressive temperament, and he kept nagging away all the time at middle and off stump, so with the turn he got he presented a problem because the batsman needed to move down the wicket if he wanted to cover the spin. That was where the Englishmen got into trouble against him.

He was a useful bat, too. Later on he captained Australia, and he was another player who put a lot back into the game as an administrator after he retired from active service.

AR Morris and SG Barnes
open the innings for
Australia.
Second Test, Sydney,
December 1946

England totalled 255. Arthur Morris and Ian Johnson,
who had gone in as nightwatchman, went fairly early,
Lindsay Hassett made 34 and Keith Miller 40, then Don
Bradman came in to join Siddy Barnes. At this stage we
were 4 for 159, so you would have to say that England
was well in the running.

AL Hassett defends.
Second Test, Sydney, 1946

DG Bradman goes out
to bat.
Second Test, Sydney, 1946

SG Barnes cuts, during his
innings of 234.
Second Test, Sydney,
December 1946

But Barnes and Bradman batted for more than a day, Bradman overtook Sid Barnes and was out for 234. The partnership of 405 for the fifth wicket is another record which Bradman still holds.

Barnes also made 234, and people have said that he gave his wicket away when he reached the same score as Bradman. Siddy was one of the great characters of the game, and always one for the provocative gesture, of course, but my view is that he seldom gave anything away, and certainly not his wicket in a Test match against England.

Australia's total was 659, 404 ahead.

Len Hutton during his
innings of 37 in the Sydney
Test, 1946

Rain again didn't help England's chances. Hutton,
often such a dour fellow, cut loose and played what
everyone who saw it still regards as one of the most
brilliant short innings ever, but he hit his wicket when
he had scored 37. Edrich made a good hundred and
Compton got a fifty, but England could only manage
371, so they went to Melbourne two down.

Covering the wicket, 1946
style.
Second Test, Sydney

Australian Prime Minister
JB Chifley and Deputy
Prime Minister HV Evatt
watching the second Test at
the Sydney Cricket Ground.
December 1946

Leader of the Opposition
RG Menzies, with
DCS Compton, at the
MCC *v* an Australian XI
match, Melbourne Cricket
Ground, November 1946

Cyril Washbrook gets Ian Johnson away behind point, during his century in the third Test, Melbourne Cricket Ground, January 1947.

The Melbourne Test was drawn. Australia made 365 and 536, England 351 and 310 for 7. The remarkable thing here was that in our first innings Colin McCool, the leg-spinner, top scored with 104, and in the second innings Don Tallon, that great wicket-keeper, made 92 and Ray Lindwall made 100, so that shows the depth of ability in the Australian team.

Arthur Morris made 155, and Cyril Washbrook made a good century in England's second innings.

Bill Voce digs one in short,
Umpire Scott calls no ball.
Bradman is surprised by the
bounce, but manages to
swing it one-handed to fine
leg. Morris backing up,
Compton at short cover.
Third Test, Melbourne,
January 1947

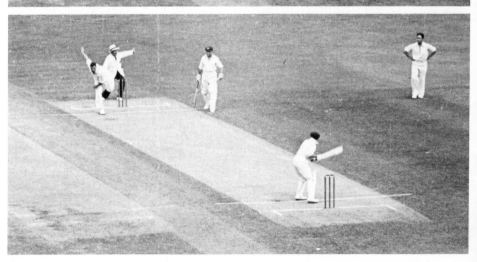

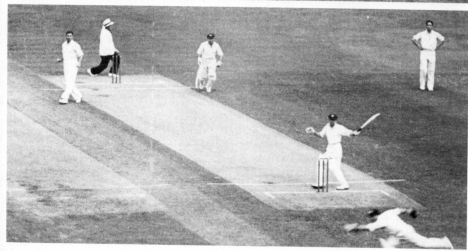

Norman Yardley has apparently deceived Bradman off the pitch, and has him caught and bowled for 49 in the third Test in Melbourne in January 1947. As ever, Bradman leaves the wicket rapidly and graciously.

CL McCool. Norman
Yardley backing up.
MCC *v* an Australian XI,
Melbourne, November 1946

So the Ashes were safe. The Adelaide pitch, as ever, was easy paced, and that Test was drawn too. Denis Compton and Arthur Morris both made centuries in each innings, and Keith Miller did exactly as he pleased with the English bowling for 141. In the final Test in Sydney Len Hutton got 122, the only century of the match, and England led on the first innings, but with Hutton unable to bat and Hammond also ill, McCool ran through the Englishmen in the second innings and Australia won by 5 wickets.

Colin McCool was one of the finds of the series, although he never went on to the great things that were predicted of him. This was to a great extent a result of the experimental rule which allowed the new ball to be

taken after 55 overs, and which was such a blow to spin bowlers everywhere. It was a tragedy for cricket that such talented cricketers as Colin McCool, George Tribe and Bruce Dooland went to England to play Lancashire League, because they knew when this rule came in that their chances of playing for Australia were over.

McCool was a hard-hitting bat, and he was a very wristy spinner who gave the ball plenty of air and plenty of spin. Like Clarrie Grimmett, Fleetwood-Smith, Doug Wright and some other names which modesty prevents me from revealing, he would have taken a power of wickets on the present cricket scene, where batsmen have never learnt the fundamentals of footwork.

Crowd on the Hill at the
Sydney Cricket Ground

In 1947–48 Bradman led Australia at home against
India, and Australia won that series four Tests to none.
The Indian side, with Amarnath the captain, Vijay
Hazare, and the tireless all-rounder Mankad, had three
really good players, but they lacked depth, they had no
fast bowlers, and they were unlucky with the weather.

| BOWLER | WKTS | RUNS |
|---|---|---|
| RANGNEKAR | | |
| ADHIKARI | | |
| KISHENCHAND | | |
| GUL MAHOMED | | |
| SARWATE | | 45 |
| NAYUDU | | 19 |
| HAZARE | | |
| AMARNATH | | 23 |
| MANKAD | | 39 |
| SOHONI | 1 | 56 |

| | |
|---|---|
| INDIA 1 INNS | 326 |
| AUS. 1ST INGS | |
| No OF OVERS | 46 |
| BATSMEN | |
| BRADMAN | 99 |
| MILLER | 59 |
| 2 FOR | 183 |

| BATSMEN | OUT | FOR W |
|---|---|---|
| BROWN | 8 | |
| ROGERS | 16 | 31 |
| WANTED AT MEMBs GATE | | |
| SUNDRIES | | |

BAR

Bradman made two centuries and a double century in the Tests, and during that tour he made his hundredth hundred in first class cricket, for an Australian XI against the Indians at the Sydney Cricket Ground. He is still the only Australian to have achieved this feat.

Sydney Cricket Ground scoreboard, India *v* an Australian XI, November 1947. Miller was to score 4 more before Bradman reached his hundredth hundred.

The hundredth run of
Bradman's hundredth
century. Kishenchand is the
bowler, Miller backing up.
Sydney Cricket Ground,
November 15, 1947

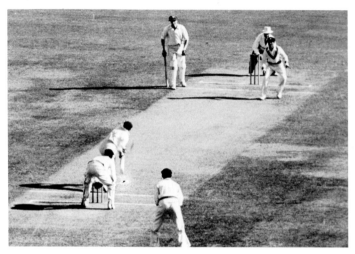

# THE GREATS OF '48

Then, in 1948, Australia went to England, where Bradman made his final appearance in that country.

The 1948 series I saw again from the very friendly vantage point of the press box, and there I assessed the importance of those five weeks the Australian team had together on board ship, where they got to know each other absolutely. These days they meet, and twenty-four hours later they are in England, and probably they still really don't know half their team mates. They were very lucky people in those old sailing days.

Don Bradman and Captain O'Sullivan on board the *Strathaird* on the way to England in 1948

Neil Harvey, Keith Miller
and Don Tallon watching
deck games on board the
*Strathaird*

Bill O'Reilly assesses the form
of the 1948 Australian touring
side. Ian Johnson behind the
stumps

WA Johnston in action
during the first Test, Trent
Bridge, June 1948

That tour, of course, was a crowning triumph for Bradman and for nearly everyone who went on the tour. The teams were pretty much the same as they had been in Australia in 1946–47, but no one would have anticipated that, apart from winning the Test rubber, they would go through the whole tour undefeated.

Bradman himself had a moderate tour by his own immoderately high standards—he was forty years of age by then—but he had developed into a tremendously thoughtful, astute captain, and he brought out the best in this young, talented side, many of whom would have been only a few years old when Bradman was making all those records in England in 1930.

How he must have enjoyed having Keith Miller and Ray Lindwall, who were both really quick and willing and able to bowl plenty of bouncers, and in 1948 in England he had Bill Johnston, the gangling Victorian left-armer with the loping run, who bowled at a good sharp pace, could seam the ball in England, and was the nicest bloke you'd meet in a day's walk. Johnston took 27 wickets in the Tests, the same number as Ray Lindwall. He could drop his pace and bowl leg spinners, too, and he did the bulk of the bowling, Miller and Lindwall being used more as shock bowlers.

Trent Bridge scoreboard at
the end of the England first
innings.
First Test, June 1948

At Trent Bridge England made only 165. Jim Laker, the
Surrey spinner, top scored with 63, Bill Johnston 5 for
36 from 25 overs. Australia replied with 509, Bradman
138 and Lindsay Hassett 137.

England's task looked hopeless, but Hutton played
another brilliant innings for 74 and then Compton,
despite a barrage of bumpers from Miller, played
probably the best innings of the series. He really took
charge, despite bad light and rain, and it looked as if
England might force a draw until he fell on his wicket at
184. Australia needed less than a hundred to win.

Crowd scene during the first
Test, Trent Bridge, June 1948

DCS Compton cuts
backward of point, and
cover drives Miller for 4,
during his innings of 184.
First Test, Trent Bridge,
June 1948

Compton was a most unusual batsman. Sometimes he would come yards down the wicket to get at a bowler, and he had a strange shot, all arms and legs, when he wanted to get the ball down to fine leg, but at other times he reminded me of Stan McCabe with the ease and timing of his shots through the covers.

He was a terrific competitor, but he was always very pleasant on the field, the ideal opponent, really.

It is always said that Compton was unorthodox, and certainly he didn't always get his feet in the right place, but batsmen come in all shapes and sizes, no two of them are much alike, in my experience. Some of the good ones are tradesmen, some are craftsmen, some, the Woolleys, the Kippaxes, the Hammonds and McCabes, are artists.

What they all have in common, the really good ones, is a sort of sublime confidence in themselves out in the middle, bred of innate ability and temperament, and years of application to their trade, or craft, or art.

Denis Compton, on his day, had this more than most.

Yardley tosses, Bradman
calls correctly.
Second Test, Lord's, June
1948

At Lord's, the second Test, Australia made 350 and 460,
England 215 and 186. Barnes and Morris made
hundreds, for England only Compton looked capable
of defying the quick bowlers.

An interesting point here was that for the third time in
a row in the Tests, Bedser had Bradman caught by
Hutton—the so-called 'Bedser-Hutton leg trap'. There
was a lot of talk about it at the time, that they might
have sorted Bradman out, but of course those of us who
knew him also knew that he hadn't come down in the
last shower and they didn't get him out there again.

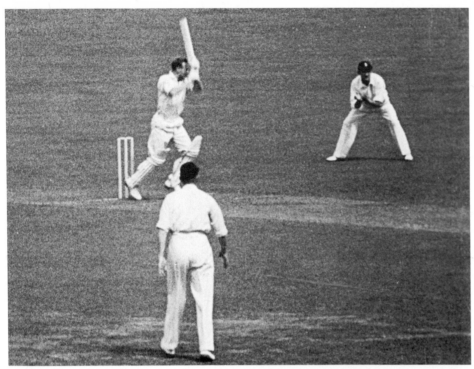

AR Morris drives through the covers off the back foot during his innings of 105. Second Test, Lord's, June 1948

Bradman facing Bedser. Godfrey Evans is behind the stumps and Len Hutton at short backward square: the 'Bedser-Hutton leg trap'. Second Test, Lord's, June 1948

Keith Miller tries to hit
Yardley out of the ground.
Godfrey Evans whips the
bails off, but Miller has his
foot back in time.
Bedser at gully, the umpire
is CN Woolley.
Second Test, Lord's, June
1948

A Coxon lbw to
ERH Toshack for 0.
Morris, Dollery, Bradman,
Miller, Umpire Davies,
Toshack, Tallon, Coxon,
Johnson, Brown, Barnes.
Second Test, Lord's, June
1948

The Old Trafford Test was drawn, Compton made another century there, and at Leeds, although England made 496, Washbrook 143 and Edrich 111, Australia replied with 458, Neil Harvey 112 in his first Test and Sam Loxton 93. England declared at 8 for 365, leaving Australia 404 to win in less than a day.

Well, in retrospect, that was a silly thing to do at Leeds, where Bradman had a Test average of nearly 200 from three previous tours. He made 173 not out, Morris 182, and Australia won with about ten minutes to spare.

So Australia went to the final Test at the Oval with three wins to nil, and all that had to be done as far as they were concerned were the tidying up operations.

One of these was Bradman's situation. We all knew, of course, that this was his last Test, but we weren't aware at the time that he only needed 4 runs to give him an average of 100 runs in Tests.

Lindwall, 6 for 20 from 16 overs, had destroyed the England batting on a wet wicket. They were all out for 52, and Barnes and Morris had an opening stand of over a hundred.

Bradman made a tremendous appearance. Everybody stood, the English team gathered out in the middle to give him three cheers, Bradman took block to a slow bowler, and I thought to myself 'Eric Hollies might get a bit of stick here'. He bowled a leg break to Bradman and it was played in the middle of the bat. Then he bowled his wrong'un. Now I don't know whether Bradman had any information about this boy bowling a wrong'un, but he bowled it, and it came back and hit the middle and leg stumps.

The whole ground was completely and utterly mes-
merised. You could have cut the silence with a knife.
Bradman was half way to the pavilion before they
realised they had to give Eric Hollies some acclamation,
and when they did they nearly knocked the stands
down, for Eric Hollies, and then for Don Bradman.
  Arthur Morris was run out 4 runs short of 200,
Australia totalled 389, and England only managed 188
in their second innings, so Australia retained the Ashes
by four Tests to nil.

Bradman bowled Hollies 0.
Fifth Test, The Oval,
August 14, 1948

That Oval Test was the end of an era. It was Bradman's last appearance in first class cricket, apart from a couple of Testimonial matches when the 1948 side came home.

Bradman had played his first Test in 1928, so he had been at the top of the cricket world for two decades, and that period had seen many great names strut across the cricket stage.

Jack Hobbs, whose name will live forever in English cricket, was still going strong when Bradman started, and many Englishmen will still argue that Jack Hobbs was the best player that ever they have seen. England had Walter Hammond too; I never bowled to a better English batsman than Hammond, and they had Maurice Leyland, a very great left-handed fighter who gave me a lot of hard times. With Herbert Sutcliffe and Len Hutton, that would make a really strong batting line up.

With their bowlers, they had Maurice Tate, God bless him, one of the finest bowlers that I ever looked at, whose career was just ending when Bradman came onto the scene. And Alec Bedser, whose career in Tests was just beginning at the end of the era, also turned out to be a very great bowler. But Harold Larwood, of course you would have to regard him as the greatest bowler of the era, no matter what you thought of bodyline. At his top, in 1932–33, and considering the batsmen he was up against, I doubt if there has ever been a better fast bowler than Larwood. There may have been one or two as good.